# WOLF
# WITHIN

## A PURGATORY NOVEL

*New York Times* and *USA Today* Bestselling Author

# CYNTHIA EDEN

# CHAPTER ONE

Special Agent Duncan McGuire raced around the street corner, chasing his prey even as his heartbeat thundered in his ears. Duncan's partner, Elias Lone, was just steps behind him. No damn way were they letting the killer escape.

The twisted bastard had already murdered four women in Seattle. Slashed their bodies. Torn out their throats. This nightmare was ending.

Duncan would make it end.

The perp rushed into an alley.

*Dead end, asshole.*

The killer didn't know the city as well as Duncan did.

His hold tightened on his weapon, and he leapt right into the entrance of that narrow alleyway. "Freeze!" Duncan roared. "FBI!"

The perp—a man with long, shaggy, blond hair—was facing the brick wall that ended the alley. At Duncan's shout, the man did freeze, for all of about twenty seconds. Then he started laughing as he spun to face Duncan and Elias.

"You humans are so out of your league," the blond snarled. His hands were up, and, as Duncan watched, the guy's nails began to transform—

Into long, black claws.

The blond laughed again. "Just the two of you? This should be so easy." His teeth were lengthening. Turning into sharp fangs. As Duncan watched, the man's face elongated. His bones snapped.

"Hell," Elias muttered from behind Duncan. "You were right. He's a wolf."

Duncan smiled, but didn't take his eyes off the killer before him. "I told you, vamps would never waste that much blood." Since Elias had just lost the bet, the guy owed him a hundred bucks. Duncan knew his werewolves.

The blond seemed to realize that they weren't exactly quaking in fear before him.

"What?" Duncan asked, lifting a brow. "Is this the part where we're supposed to act shocked because you can grow fur and howl at the moon?"

"You fuckin'—"

"Sorry," Duncan muttered, "but you're hardly the first Para that we've taken down." Actually, Duncan and Elias were part of an elite unit that *only* hunted the paranormals in Seattle. The paranormals usually hid in plain sight, mostly managing to pass for humans.

Until they started to *eat* said humans. When the vampires and werewolves went bad and humans wound up as their prey of choice, well, that was when Duncan came in.

Someone had to keep the humans safe.

Duncan's words seemed to enrage the werewolf before him. The guy's lips peeled back—yeah, those teeth and claws were the weapons that had ended the lives of those four co-eds—and the fellow's body stretched as the power of the shift flooded through him.

Duncan kept his own body loose and ready. His gun was in his hand, but he wasn't firing unless the werewolf attacked him. His orders were to take the werewolf in, not to kill him.

The werewolf's elongated teeth snapped together.

*Like I haven't seen all this shit before.*

Unlike most humans, Duncan knew the score about the supernaturals. He'd known the truth since he'd been a kid.

"Humans aren't going to stop me!" The killer's cry was guttural. "You can't!" Fur burst along his skin. He fell to the ground, his knees and palms hitting the cement. His eyes glowed. "You don't have the power!" That last was more growl than human speech as the guy completed his shift...

And became a full-on wolf.

The wolf launched at Duncan. *Not coming in alive.* Duncan's fingers tightened around the trigger. He fired. Once. Twice.

The bullets stopped the werewolf cold.

"Silver, dumbass," Duncan said with a sad shake of his head as smoke drifted from the wolf's body. "It'll stop your kind every time." The fur slowly melted from the beast's body. The bones reshaped. In death, the monster became a man again. Well, not completely a man. A werewolf still kept his fangs and claws at death.

"Nice shots," Elias said, still from behind him.

Duncan grunted. He kept his weapon up as he eased closer to the body. Lowering the gun at this point would be a rookie mistake. Paras weren't like humans. Even if they *looked* dead, half the time, they weren't. They'd keep coming and coming and coming, just like the monsters in scary movies. Only this wasn't a movie.

Reality was scarier than the late-night horror shows.

"You hit him in the head," Elias said as he slid closer. "Don't worry, man, he's gone. He's—"

A growl sounded from the mouth of the alley. Duncan spun around.

Too late.

It wasn't just a lone werewolf they were hunting. He'd thought they were dealing with an isolated killer, a werewolf gone mad with bloodlust. That profile had been what the intel had showed him.

The intel was wrong.

Logan was gazing at a pack. Four other fully shifted werewolves were at the front of that alley.

They were leaping for Elias. And Elias had put up his weapon already. *Rookie mistake.*

Duncan rushed forward and shoved his partner to the side, barely dodging the claws of a werewolf. Duncan aimed his gun and started firing. Again and again.

One wolf down. Another—

He felt teeth tear into his shoulder.

Into his neck.

He could smell the wild, woodsy scent of the beasts. His own blood. He could *feel* his blood, trailing down his neck, soaking his shirt.

His gun wasn't firing. He'd used all the bullets.

More wolves were closing in...

Just as they'd closed in when he'd been four. When they'd killed his family.

When he'd lost everything but his life.

He hadn't been able to see the wolves then, but he'd heard their snarls and his mother's desperate cries. He could still hear those cries in his nightmares.

She hadn't survived the attack.

He had.

Only this time, Duncan knew he wouldn't be so lucky.

Elias was screaming. The beasts were howling.

And Duncan—Duncan was pretty sure that he was dying.

\*\*\*

"I'm so sorry, man." Elias's voice was shaking and miserable.

Duncan opened his eyes. Pain knifed through him. Twisting. Gutting him.

He tried to move. Couldn't.

Not because of the pain but because...because he was strapped down?

*What the hell?*

"I'm sorry," Elias said again.

Duncan's gaze flew to the other man. Elias stood a few feet away, and the faint glow from a streetlight revealed the haggard appearance of his face.

Why was Elias apologizing? They'd both made it out of that stinking alley, and, wonder of wonders, they were both actually still breathing. "You...owe me..." Duncan managed.

Elias shook his head. The lines on his face deepened even more.

"Get him to the containment facility," a hard voice ordered.

Whoa...what? *Containment?* Containment was where his team—the Seattle division of the FBI's not-supposed-to-exist Para Unit—sent their captured *shifters* and vampires for temporary holding. He wasn't a prisoner. He was one of the *good* guys.

Duncan tried to lift his head. On the second attempt, he actually succeeded, and it was then that he saw the face of his boss, Eric Pate, come into focus. "I'm sorry," Pate said, and he actually sounded like he was, odd for the usually emotionless director, "but we don't have an option."

Duncan jerked at the bonds holding him down. The other agents had strapped him to a gurney and were wheeling him toward a waiting ambulance.

"You were bitten by the suspect." Real regret tinged Pate's voice. "You know what that means."

*Bitten.* No. The fuck, *no.* "Kill me," Duncan snapped. Because there was no way he'd become a monster. The werewolves only existed to torture and kill. To slaughter. Their beasts dominated. They attacked anyone and everything.

Just like they'd attacked his family.

*I won't be like that.* When he'd agreed to become part of the secret division, he'd known there would be deadly risks involved in his cases.

He'd known the risks, and he'd long ago decided what he would and wouldn't become.

"No!" Elias yelled as he surged forward. "Pate, dammit, don't! You promised—"

Screw any promises that Pate had made to Elias. Now Duncan remembered the feel of teeth tearing into his flesh. His neck. His shoulder. With all of those bites and the blood loss, he *should* be dead.

But he wasn't. Because his body was already transforming.

If a werewolf's bite didn't kill you...if you had the DNA that would enable you to become a beast, then just one bite from a shifted werewolf would infect you. Transform you.

*I don't want to be—*

"If you go rogue, I'll put a silver bullet in your head myself," Pate promised, green eyes glittering. *Rogue.* That was the term for werewolves who couldn't maintain their control. They lost all touch with humanity. *Beasts.* Monsters. Pate's gaze stayed locked on Duncan as the guy continued, "But you're one of us, and *no one* is putting you down yet. We're damn well going to give you a chance at survival first."

Pate didn't understand. He didn't get it. He was a suit who saw the wolves from a distance. Duncan had seen the newly transformed up close and personal. The beast took over. It was all basic instinct. All need and bloodlust.

Pate looked up and nodded toward the agents around Duncan. "Take him to Holly. She can take care of his wounds and start to get a read on him—"

He snarled. Duncan's body twisted and a fire seemed to burn beneath his skin. "Not...her..."

The boss didn't know how Duncan felt for the pretty, little doctor. Holly was already his temptation with her sweet smelling skin and her fuck-me eyes. He'd tried to stay away because he'd known she was too fragile to handle someone like him.

If she hadn't been able to handle the man he'd been, there was no way she'd be safe around his soon-to-be-emerging werewolf side.

"He's starting to change!" Elias's shout. "Drug him and get the guy in that ambulance!"

A needle shoved into his arm.

Duncan kept fighting and trying to get them to understand, "Not...Hol..."

They were loading him into the ambulance. They weren't *listening* to him. Holly was the last person he should be around. He wanted her as a man. He knew that a werewolf's desires were just magnified.

And what the wolf wanted, he took.

Without thought. Without remorse.

No limits. No control. No conscience.

Just the beast.

He opened his mouth and only a growl escaped. *Not Holly. Keep me away from her. I'll hurt her.*

He could feel the fire spreading beneath his skin. Hands were on him, holding Duncan down because the drug wasn't working.

"Uh, is he supposed to be this strong?" One of the agents—Shane, he knew Shane, they played cards every Wednesday—asked nervously. "Cause this hoss is—"

The strap across his chest broke free, and Duncan lunged up.

*Not Holly!*

Another needle was jabbed into his neck. One straight into his heart.

"That'll stop a tiger," Pate panted out the words.

A tiger...

Or a werewolf.

Duncan fell back against the gurney.

*Holly, I'm sorry.*

His eyes closed.

\*\*\*

Holly Young gasped when the doors to her medical wing were shoved open. She had been packing up, ready to go home for a few hours of chilling on the couch and watching crime TV reruns but—

"Holly, an agent was bitten!"

She snapped to attention. Everyone in their division knew the risks of the job. When they started hunting monsters, they'd all realized that the agents faced the risk of one day *becoming* a monster. Of getting exposed.

*Bitten.*

She yanked on her gloves even as she motioned toward the operating table on her right. "Put him there, and let me check him out." Her heart was racing, but her hands were rock-steady. "What are we dealing with?" Holly asked as she rushed forward. The agent was strapped down. Unmoving. She couldn't see who it was. There were over two dozen agents in Seattle's Para Unit.

"Multiple werewolf bites," Pate told her.

*Multiple.* She gulped. "You know what's happening to him. He'll die from the poison in those bites." There wasn't much she could do for a werewolf bite. If the agent had been bitten by a vampire, she could have given him a transfusion, made sure the wound was closed. Possibly saved him.

But a werewolf bite?

Death sentence.

"He's *not* dying." Pate stared at her with narrowed eyes. "The agent has already started to transform."

She almost dropped her stethoscope at that news.

A human transforming into a werewolf? That was so rare.

And deadly.

Her heart drummed even faster in her chest, and her hands gave the slightest tremble as she hurried toward the table. The other agents had transferred the wounded man onto the table she'd indicated, and they had already strapped him down once more. Holly elbowed them aside, trying to make her way through to see the poor agent who'd just been given a one-way ticket to hell.

She saw his dark hair first. Thick and a little too long. Then her gaze fell to his strong cheekbones, knife sharp. She recognized the hard blade of his nose, but his eyes were closed, so she didn't see his normal bright blue stare.

*Duncan?*

"Get back," Pate ordered the other agents as he lifted his hands. "Clear the room so she can work!" Then Pate's fingers curled around her elbow, and he leaned in close to her. His voice lowered as he whispered, "You keep him sane." An order. Or a plea?

She stared down at Duncan's powerful body. Blood was all over him. Already drying on his ripped clothes. On his neck. His arms. But even as she stared at him, the long, thick gashes on his body were closing before her eyes.

Werewolf healing. That was some kind of magic.

"He's going to be very strong," Pate murmured, the soft words just for her ears. The other agents had already backed up. Backed up, but she noticed that Duncan's partner, Elias, still had his gun out.

And aimed at Duncan's unconscious body.

She moved her own body a few inches, deliberately putting herself in the line of fire. *You aren't shooting him!*

"We can use him," Pate said, his body brushing against hers. "If we can control him, then this could be our chance."

This wasn't a chance. It was a man's life.

She reached out her hand to touch Duncan's skin. Even through her glove, she could feel the heat pouring off his body.

"Clear the room!" Pate snarled again. Because the other agents were lingering. She didn't blame them. One of their own had just been taken down in a way that was no doubt a nightmare fear for them all.

"But, sir..." Elias stepped forward. *And he still had his gun out.* "He's too dangerous to leave alone with her! He could attack—"

Pate's shaking head stopped his words. "He's not going to wake up for hours. And by then, he'll be collared."

*Collared.* When werewolves were brought in for containment at the facility, the first order of business was always to suit them up with a silver collar. The collar controlled them. Kept them in check every moment. If the werewolves tried to attack anyone, then silver was automatically released from those collars and injected into their blood via tiny needles.

The collars themselves were unbreakable, mostly because they were *made* of silver, and no werewolf had ever been strong enough to fight the silver and escape.

The old story about silver being the weakness for the wolf? Luckily for humans, that story had turned out to be true. If the werewolves hadn't been given some sort of weakness, the humans would be screwed.

But the idea of Duncan...collared like that...

Her back teeth clenched.

"He doesn't *want* this," Elias shouted.

That gun of his needed to be holstered. She was about to do it for him.

"Right now, the man doesn't know what he wants!" Pate threw back. Holly knew Pate wouldn't back down. He never did. "Now, Agent

Lone, I'm ordering you to stand down. This isn't your call. And it isn't his, either."

Because once you joined the Para Unit, your life wasn't exactly your own any longer.

Swearing, Elias holstered his weapon. Finally. Then he turned on his heel and hurried from the room. The double doors swung shut behind him.

Holly forced herself to take in a deep breath. Duncan had been viciously attacked, and now, to come back as a werewolf? Pate had taken risks before with his agents, but there had never been a case like this.

"He's going to be an alpha," Pate whispered, staying close to her so his words wouldn't carry far. She knew the other agents were waiting just outside of the medical wing. "I can tell by the speed of his healing. Hell, the guy was already starting to shift at the scene. We had to dose him three times just to stop the change."

*Three times?* She'd been the one to brew that drug. Holly knew it was powerful. One dose should have been more than enough to put Duncan out.

The doors to her medical wing flew open again, and she jerked. Elias—coming back? What the hell?

His cheeks were flushed. His blond hair mussed. He pointed toward Holly. "She's going to need a guard in here with her!" Elias called out. "The doc won't be able to handle him."

Shane August grabbed Elias and tried to yank him back. Elias didn't appear in the mood to be yanked.

Pate exhaled slowly. "After Duncan has the collar on, she'll be able to control him." Then Pate pointed to Shane. "August, you stay in here and keep an eye on Holly until she has Duncan secure."

Shane, not Elias. Very good choice.

Shane shoved Elias back of the room, then he stood there, near the door, with his watchful brown gaze locked on Duncan's body.

Pate made no move to leave, not yet. "Check him out, top to bottom. Get blood work. Run your tests. Every test you can think of."

Tests that would show them all just how deadly Duncan would become.

She nodded and met Pate's stare. "If he—if he proves to be too much of a threat?" Because she'd seen werewolves who had no sense of humanity left in them. Beasts that couldn't be controlled or contained. They'd all seen wolves like that. In her experience, those recently bitten were the worst.

The most dangerous.

"Then *you* stop him." She noticed the emphasis he put in his command. "But that's a last resort. I don't want to lose him. We need him, Holly. We need what he'll become."

Because while the other agents thought that Pate was just a suit who never got his hands dirty, she knew better. Pate had been chosen to lead the West Coast Para Unit because he knew all about the dark side of life.

And he also believed that the best way to fight a monster was...with a monster.

That was why she was there.

"Do whatever you have to do, but make sure Duncan McGuire survives." Then Pate was backing away. He crossed to Shane's side, whispered to the agent, and after a moment, the swinging doors to the med room closed behind Pate.

She didn't move from her position near Duncan. *Duncan McGuire.* He'd always made her nervous. Too aware.

She put on her stethoscope. Bent to listen to his heartbeat. *So fast.* Not weak, the way it should have been considering the amount of drugs in his system. Duncan's heartbeat was thundering at a frantic rate.

*The transformation.*

Holly had been hired to be the personal physician for the agents in the Para Unit. When you went out and fought monsters, you could return with some rather...unusual wounds. Instead of explaining vamp bites and shifter claw marks to the local hospital staff, Pate had wanted her to take care of his men and women.

He'd also wanted her to study the prisoners in containment.

Two reasons to bring her in. There were more reasons, of course, there always were. But those were the two he'd used to the FBI Brass.

And, since she'd owed Pate far more than she could ever repay, it wasn't like Holly had been given much of a choice in taking the job.

No, she'd lost that whole choice option a year ago. When she'd lost her life.

Carefully now, she lifted one of Duncan's eyelids. She was about to shine her light on his eye when she realized—

*No need for the light.*

His eye was shining on its own. The blue had lit up, streaking with gold. *Already a werewolf's sight.* A werewolf's vision was ten times better than a human's during the day, and at night, werewolves could *see* in the darkness. All of a werewolf's senses were enhanced. Incredibly amped.

She backed away from him a bit. Her gaze scanned over his body. *So much blood.* Her nostrils flared at the scent. Considering the damage he'd sustained, it was amazing that he'd survived the attack.

And if he hadn't? If Pate had come back to tell her that Duncan had died on his mission? How would she have felt then?

Holly swallowed. She put down the small light, and her gloved hands reached out to skim over the wound on his neck. *I would have missed you.*

She'd been paying too much attention to Duncan from the very beginning. On her second day at the facility, he'd walked in with a bullet in his shoulder. He'd stripped off his shirt. She'd dug the bullet out, been all business.

Until she'd looked up and gotten caught by his bright, blue gaze.

As a rule, when she looked at Duncan, Holly wanted. She craved.

Dangerous, but then, Duncan was a dangerous man. He was about to become even more so.

"Shane..." She raised her voice so the agent near the door would hear her. "Please get me the silver collar from the storage room."

"I'm supposed to guard—" Shane began, his voice rumbling just a little with the drawl of South Carolina.

Holly glanced up at him. Shane was a good guy. Tall, blond, with classic features and warm, brown eyes. Handsome, no doubt appealing to most women.

She wasn't most. She didn't want pretty boy perfect.

Her fingers lightly skimmed over Duncan's shoulder. "He's out. Don't worry, I'll be fine. Just...get the collar for me, will you?"

After one last worried glance at Duncan's still figure, Shane headed toward the storage room.

Her breath eased out on a relieved exhale.

*Good.* She'd wanted a few moments alone with Duncan. She reached for her scissors. Carefully, Holly cut away his shirt. She bagged it and sealed it because Pate would want an analysis done on all that blood.

Then she bent to inspect the bites on Duncan's neck and shoulder. "They sure tore into you," she whispered. But those wounds were closing. Already healing as he became something far more than man. "I'm so sorry, Duncan."

She'd barely talked to him before this attack. Too nervous. Every time his eyes had locked on her, Holly's heartbeat had kicked up and raced in her chest. She'd stuttered and glanced away because—

*I want him.* Only, before, he wouldn't have been able to handle her secrets. No man could.

Not and keep living, anyway.

Almost helplessly, her hands slid over the muscles of his chest. The shift would make his muscles harder, even more defined. Not just a six pack anymore, hell, it looked like he was close to getting a dang twelve pack—

His hand flew up. His fingers wrapped around her wrist, holding her far too tightly.

Holly's gaze jerked to his face. His eyes were wide open, the gold even bolder in that blue gaze that it had been moments before. His lips were parted, and she could just see the edge of his lengthening canines.

*Oh, hell.* "Duncan?"

He jerked to a sitting position, snapping those straps that had been over his body in an instant, and he yanked her closer to him. His other hand rose and wrapped around her shoulder, effectively trapping her in place.

His brows lowered as he studied her, and his nostrils widened as if he were drinking in her scent.

*Not good.*

"D-Duncan, you're back at the med unit. I'm just checking you over to make sure—"

His head lowered toward her throat. Holly yelped, thinking he was going for her jugular, and she tried to push him back.

Only there was no pushing him.

*Enhanced strength, definite check.* It sure looked like Pate was right about the alpha coming out in Duncan.

*He was right.*

*And I could be screwed.*

Her nails sank into his shoulders. She didn't want to hurt him. He'd been hurt enough. But...

He wasn't biting her. Wasn't sinking those new, wickedly sharp canines of his into her neck. He was—

Nuzzling her? What. The. Hell?

Holly was pretty sure that she'd just felt the lick of his tongue over her neck.

She shuddered against him. "Ah...Duncan...you need to let me go...I can help you..."

He was on the edge of the table now. He'd pulled her between his legs. Caged her so well. The heat from his body scorched her.

His right hand wasn't on her shoulder any longer. It had just dropped to the curve of her ass.

*"Duncan!"* Her voice snapped at him.

His head lifted. Only the man she'd known wasn't staring back at her from those gold/blue eyes. A hungry beast stared back at her. A beast who sure looked like he was ready for a bite.

*Been there, done that.*

His burning gaze seemed to consume her. *"Want..."* The word was an inhuman rasp, a beast's growl.

"You..." Holly paused, wet her too-dry lips and muttered, "need to let me go—"

Her mouth was still open when his lips crashed down on hers. Not gentle. Not even close.

Desperate and rough and wild. His tongue thrust into her mouth. His hold tightened around her, and Duncan—

*Took.*

She'd wondered what it would be like to kiss Duncan McGuire. She'd daydreamed. Fantasized. Harmless thoughts, really.

She'd never imagined anything like this. His tongue thrust into her mouth. His tongue tasted and tempted. His tight hold had her pressed hard to the front of his body, and there was no missing his arousal.

Um, no missing it at all.

She shouldn't respond. He was injured. Probably out of his mind from the transformation mutating within him, but the hot touch of his mouth on hers seemed to send a current of pleasure right through Holly's body. Her breasts tightened. Her hips pushed restlessly against the thick length of his cock and—

"Dr. Young!" Shane's horrified voice cut through the cloud of lust.

*Shane.* And, just like that, Holly didn't have to worry about breaking free of Duncan's grip. Because at the other man's shout, Duncan pushed her away from him and leapt from the table.

Then he went after Shane. With claws stretching from the tips of his fingers and with a snarl on his lips, Duncan launched at the other man.

"*No!*" Holly screamed.

But Duncan didn't stop. Shane had the silver collar in his hands, and he'd holstered his weapon, so he had to drop the collar before he could arm himself.

The collar hit the floor, and Shane didn't move fast enough to draw out his weapon.

Duncan's right hand wrapped around Shane's throat. He lifted the agent up into the air. Shane's feet dangled, and he tried to choke out some speech.

*We are so screwed.* She'd been right earlier. "Duncan! Let him go!" Holly screamed. He hadn't hurt her, but it certainly looked like he was ready to introduce Shane to a whole world of pain.

Wolves were territorial. *Especially* the alphas. Duncan had been coming on to her— *marking* her in the way of shifters, she knew that—and then another male had come into the room.

*So screwed.*

Shane was struggling to get out his gun. His fingers were shaking, but, on the third try, he managed to yank the weapon from the holster. Then Shane tried to lift the gun to Duncan's chest.

"*No!*" Now her scream was full of fear. She raced toward them.

But, with his left hand, Duncan just snatched away the gun and tossed it across the room. "*Stay away...*" Duncan snarled as he lifted Shane higher, "*from her.*"

Holly grabbed the collar. Unlocked it. Duncan was so tall, about six foot four, and she was only five foot seven, so this was gonna be tricky. She jumped up, trying to latch on around his back.

He spun at once, slamming Shane to the floor and catching her in his arms. He lifted her, bringing her closer even as he frowned down at her.

*Gotcha.*

"Sorry," Holly whispered, and she locked the collar around his throat. The silver immediately began to burn him, sending faint plumes of smoke into the air as the skin on his neck reddened and blistered.

He dropped her, and her ass hit the tile with an impact that would leave one hell of a bruise. But she jumped to her feet and rushed toward the counter. Duncan was yelling and snarling and trying to yank the silver collar away from his neck.

"Stop!" Holly shouted at him as her fingers curled around the collar's remote. "You're just making it hurt worse!" That was the way the collar had been designed. The more you struggled, the more you'd burn.

She typed in a code for that collar, then adjusted the setting, knocking down the intensity. "Give me just a second, and I'll help you."

His head whipped toward her. His fingers were still at the collar, shaking. Burning.

"I can make the pain stop," she whispered, "but you have to show me that you have control."

He was coming toward her. Stalking her. Seemingly uncaring now of the burns on his throat.

"D-Duncan?"

He kept coming toward her. Holly was afraid that "control" might not be part of his vocabulary anymore.

# CHAPTER TWO

Footsteps thundered behind him. "Freeze, McGuire!"

*Freeze.* The order was so familiar. So was the voice shouting it. Pate.

But Duncan didn't freeze. He kept stalking toward Holly. She was the only thing that mattered to him.

Holly with her high cheekbones, those deep, dark brown eyes, her golden skin, and the dark silk of her hair.

Why hadn't he ever noticed how sweet she smelled? Her scent was pulling him in, drawing him closer and closer.

He'd followed that scent on her neck. Tasted her skin with his tongue.

She tasted as sweet as she smelled.

He'd taken her lips. Enjoyed her mouth. Her lips were red from his kiss now, and all he could think was...

*I want to taste all of her.*

The beast was growling, eager to claim his prey.

"*Don't take another step, McGuire!*" That annoying voice shouted again. "*Or I'll shoot!*"

The swinging doors burst open behind Pate.

Duncan didn't have to take another step. Holly was the one who rushed toward him. She hurried to stand between him...and the group of agents who'd just rushed into the med unit.

The armed agents.

Duncan's gaze swept over them. When he'd first awoken, he'd known only lust. For Holly. He'd seen her. Smelled her. Wanted.

Then Shane had come in, and all he'd been able to think was...*Stay away*. A haze of red had covered his vision. *Mine*. An instinctive, primal response.

But the silver collar was doing its job. It was keeping the wolf in check. Holding back the beast.

*For now*. The sinister whisper seemed to come from within him.

His gaze swept over the agents. Pate's face was tense. He'd clenched his jaw, and the guy's green gaze glittered.

Elias, the poor bastard, looked miserable. He was pale, with a stricken stare.

Shane had picked himself off the floor and was rolling his right shoulder. *Huh. Did I dislocate it?* Maybe. Things had been a little hazy at that point.

Three other agents were behind them—Daphne, Brent, and Luke. All of their weapons were aimed at Duncan and, now, at Holly.

*The weapons were pointed at Holly.*

He lifted his hands. Saw the long, deadly black claws that had sprung from his fingertips.

"Everyone needs to calm down," Holly said, but her own voice was shaking and high. "He's collared. He's under control."

*Collared.* He barely felt the burn of the silver on his neck anymore. Or the burn in his fingers. He just felt—

*Strong.* Like he could rip apart anyone who got in his way.

Maybe he would.

"He doesn't seem controlled to me," Shane muttered, rolling that shoulder once more. "He nearly choked the life out of me!"

There were red imprints on Shane's neck.

*From my hands.*

Duncan took a step back. Stared harder at his claws. He hadn't wanted this. Hadn't *ever* wanted it.

He looked up—and right into Elias's gaze.

"I'm sorry," his partner whispered the words, but Duncan heard him perfectly.

Because his senses were enhanced.

He wasn't human anymore.

He grabbed Holly's arm and spun her toward him. "What the fuck is happening?"

Her eyes widened.

The others started to spring forward.

"Stop!" Holly yelled, and she threw out one hand, palm out, to halt them in their tracks. "He's not attacking me. Duncan is in control." Then, softer, just for his ears, she said, "Please, tell me that you're in control."

*Her scent...* His head bent toward her. He wanted to bite. Badly. But he managed, "I'm in...control." *Lie.*

"Good." Her breath rushed out. "Pate, get your agents to lower their guns! Duncan is contained. There's no need for any more violence."

"He *choked* me—" Shane snapped.

"But he didn't kill you," Holly threw back without taking her gaze off Duncan's. "You're lucky. He'd just woken up, his beast was in command."

"And what?" Shane demanded, his faint drawl thickening a bit. "His beast wanted to fuck? 'Cause it sure looked like he was about to eat you alive."

Her cheeks flushed a dark red. Duncan's head whipped up, and his eyes locked on the other agent.

Shane immediately stumbled back. "Wow, big guy. Easy. Let's not go for my throat again, okay?"

The thought was tempting.

"McGuire?" Pate called. "Are you in control or is that wolf about to launch out?"

Gritting his teeth Duncan said, "I'm...here." *A monster. Fucking claws and fangs and a fire burning beneath my skin.*

"Good," Pate said as he holstered his gun. His gaze swept over Duncan. Then Holly. "But are you gonna stay in control?"

That was hard to say. Duncan didn't know if he'd even give that one fifty-fifty odds.

"Get your men out of here," Holly urged, voice stronger now, as she darted a glance at Pate. "I need to finish my exam on Duncan."

"It's *not* safe," Shane immediately fired. "Duncan can go beast any minute!"

"Not with the silver on him," Holly said, shaking her head. Her hair slipped back over her shoulders. "Just at this facility, we've used the collars on over three dozen werewolf prisoners at various times, and they all stayed in human form with them on." She looked back up at Duncan. "As long as the collar is on, they can't shift fully. The collar will keep him in check."

Did the others hear the faint hitch in her words? A dead giveaway for a lie.

But, no, Pate was nodding his head. Motioning for the others to file out. With slumped shoulders, Elias was the first agent out the door. The others followed suit, with Shane casting a few suspicious glances over his shoulder as he left.

Then only Pate was there. His gaze studied Duncan like he was some kind of damn experiment. *Oh, yeah, I am.*

"Finish the exam, then..." Pate's jaw clenched. "I'm sorry, McGuire, but you'll have to stay in a cell for tonight. Just until we're absolutely sure about you. We can't—"

*Can't turn me loose on the humans.*

Right. He knew what happened when a wild werewolf attacked.

He stared down at his claws. The damn things wouldn't retract.

"Holly?" Pate motioned for her to come closer. Slowly, Holly left Duncan's side. He noticed that she kept the collar's remote in her hand. Probably in case he went wild, and she needed to zap him with a high dose of silver.

Pate bent his head near hers. His fingers slid over her shoulder.

Duncan growled.

Pate's head immediately lifted, and he frowned at Duncan.

"*Don't touch her,*" Duncan ordered, voice lethal. The wolf was suddenly right there, beneath his skin. He could smell Holly, and now...now Pate's thick scent was mingling with hers.

*Away. Away from her. Now.*

Pate backed up a step. "I was afraid that would happen." He shook his head. "It's the reason I wanted you away from the other wolves, Holly. I told you that it was a good idea for your assistant to take the blood samples from them." Pate tapped his nose. "He's reacting to what you are."

What she was?

Holly darted a quick glance at Duncan. "I can help him. You know I can. Just...give me time."

Since she was looking at Duncan, Holly missed the calculating gaze that Pate gave her.

Duncan didn't miss it, and he wondered what game Pate was playing.

"Don't be afraid to amp up that silver," Pate advised her. Then he was gazing at Duncan once more. "I know you're angry."

Duncan laughed. A bitter, twisted sound. "I knew...the risks coming in..." Talking seemed hard. As if it were some foreign activity, and his voice was rougher and deeper than it had been before. "But I told you...*always*...I never wanted to be like this..."

"Most would have died from your injuries, McGuire. You know that only about one percent of the population can even become werewolves."

One percent. The deadliest one percent. Men and women with DNA that had designed them to be perfect killers. Men and women who were skilled at hunting, at dealing death.

*I was too good at my job.*

"Not everyone can track wolves the way you did, moving almost as damn fast as them," Pate continued.

Duncan shoved his claws behind his back.

"Now we need to see just what you'll become—"

Duncan laughed. "I'll *become* a monster, you know it. I know it." He inclined his head toward Holly. "She knows it. The collar will hold me for now, but what the hell happens when the full moon rises and I turn?" Because all werewolves shifted into the form of the beast when the moon rose. During the rise of the full moon, a werewolf was at his strongest, most dangerous point. "You just gonna keep me locked up forever? Because that's what you'd have to do. If you let me out, I'll kill."

"One step at a time," Pate said, voice flat. "The moon won't rise for a few days."

That wasn't exactly a whole lot of time.

"A lot can happen between now and then."

Yeah, things changed fast all right. Just yesterday, he'd been a human with a hard-on for the sexy little doc who stood just a few feet away. Now, he was a werewolf.

And he still wanted her.

Pate cut his gaze toward Holly. "Give me your report as soon as you're done examining him."

"Right."

Then Pate was gone. The fool actually left Holly alone with him.

Holly stared after Pate a moment, then she headed toward those swinging doors that led out of the med unit. She punched in a series of numbers on the keypad near the left door.

A bolt slid into place, locking her and Duncan in the room. Locking the others out.

"You sure that's...wise?" Duncan muttered. "You just locked yourself in—"

"With a big, bad werewolf?" Holly finished and turned toward him. Surprisingly, there was no fear in her eyes. "Don't worry, I can handle you."

Because she still had her little fingers curved around the remote. "And what if the silver stops working?" That tiny little remote didn't seem so all powerful to him.

Her gaze went to his neck. "Then I'll come up with a Plan B. I'm pretty good at coming up with backup plans."

He wanted to smile. If his life hadn't gone straight to hell, he probably would have. "You're too smart for this. You know that you need to get away from me."

The woman who'd spent so long blushing and avoiding his gaze now tilted her head back and stared him *straight* in the eyes. Then she began to walk toward him with slow, but sure steps. "Why? Because you might decide to take a bite out of me again?"

He'd be honest. "Because I don't have a whole lot of control right now, and, doc, in case you missed the little show earlier, I want to fuck you."

The blunt words made her hesitate, just for a moment. She rallied pretty quickly though. "I...um...didn't miss it, no." Holly motioned to the table behind him. He glanced back at the straps he'd shredded. Duncan didn't really recall ripping them apart. "Can you get back on the table? I need to finish my exam."

Because he was the new science project in the Para Unit. He turned away from her and faced the table. She closed the distance between them, the clicks of her high heels filling his ears and her seductive scent wrapping around him. "*Dammit.*" His hands slammed down, and his fingers curled around the side of the exam table. He was pretty sure that he was about to dent the metal.

"What is it?" Then she made a mistake. She touched him.

He whirled toward her and grabbed her hand. *Careful, careful.* Her wrist felt so delicate in his grasp that he was afraid one wrong move from him would shatter her bones.

"Why do you smell like that?" Duncan demanded as he inhaled deeply, desperate for more of her scent.

Her eyes were wide. Darker than the night. "Like what?" Her voice came out as a husky whisper. The kind of whisper a woman used when she was in bed.

"Like honey and sex. Sin. Fucking temptation." And resisting temptation was becoming harder with every second that passed.

She tried to pull her hand away. "I-I don't know what you mean."

Her scent was driving him crazy. His temples began to throb. So did another part of his body.

"Your senses are heightened. All werewolves have sharper senses than humans. So maybe my...ah...scent just seems different to you because of that."

Maybe. But he was also starting to think her sweet scent might be making him a bit drunk.

When she tried to break free again, he let her go.

She quickly put about three feet of space between them.

And he realized that she still had the remote in her left hand. "Why...why didn't you use the collar?"

She gave a faint laugh. The sound slid right over his skin like a caress. "Because you caught my hand? Duncan, you'd have to do a whole lot more to me than just that. I'm not going to hurt you for a touch."

But he wanted far more than a touch.

"Climb onto the table," she said, her voice still with a faint huskiness that he liked too much. "Let me finish my exam. I need to get some blood samples. Check your wounds."

"I don't have any wounds." The truth. He'd felt the skin stretching. Mending.

Any wounds that he'd gotten during his attack were gone.

"Werewolves don't usually heal that fast," she said, brows pulling low. Holly attached the collar's remote to her belt, then she came forward once more and put her hands on his chest as she studied his body.

Her hands were slightly cool. Her touch was probably meant to be the impersonal one of a doctor but...

He had to grind his back teeth together to hold back a moan.

"They're totally healed. Amazing." She reached for a needle. Pushed it against the vein near his elbow. The needle snapped. "I was afraid of that." She reached around him. Lifted a second syringe. "This needle has silver elements in its composition. It will penetrate your skin, but it'll hurt." Her lips tightened. "It'll burn."

He appreciated the warning, but... "I'm already burning."

Her gaze snapped up to his. "What?"

"It feels like my blood is boiling. Everything is heating inside me." He waved his hand. "So drive the damn needle in me. It won't make any difference."

She bit her lip. *I want to bite it.* Instead, he yanked his gaze away from her. Tried to look anywhere, but at her. Because he didn't want her to see the wild lust in his gaze.

The needle pushed into his arm. Yeah, he barely felt that little sting.

Then she was pulling the needle out. Rubbing his arm lightly with her gloved fingers.

"*Stop.*" Because he couldn't handle anymore. The beast was snarling inside of him, and the silver collar didn't seem to be holding the wolf in check much.

*Want.*

It was her scent. Honey and sex. Calling to him. Tempting.

*Kiss her. Strip her.*

*Fuck her.*

"Am I hurting you?" Her voice was that soft murmur that she'd probably use after sex.

"Get. Away," Duncan gritted. Because his claws were still out. If he touched her again, he'd hurt her. Cut her skin. Make her bleed.

*Wasn't that what monsters did? And hadn't he become a monster?*

"I-I didn't mean to hurt you." She stumbled back and her elbow banged into an instrument tray.

"You didn't hurt me." He held his body perfectly still, fighting the urge to literally pounce on her. "But if you don't get away from me, I'll hurt you."

He knew a containment cell was down the hallway to the left. Cell A was separated from the other prisoners.

"Go unbar the door and let me out." Definitely more animal growl then.

"Where will you go?"

"Cell A." Maximum security.

She hurried toward the door. A few seconds later, the bar slid back. He didn't look at her as he nearly ran out of the med unit. He had to get to Cell A. Had to be contained. Before it was too late.

His cock was aching. His muscles trembling. And if she came close to him again, with that scent, with those dark eyes...

*I will hurt her.*

Because it wasn't just the man who wanted her. He'd been right about that fear. The beast he was becoming wanted her, too.

Maybe he wanted her even more.

"Duncan!" She was rushing after him. He didn't stop. He entered Cell A. Slammed the door behind him. Then he took five quick steps away from the door.

Her breath was panting out. Her breasts rising and falling.

"Lock it," he snarled.

"What's happening? Are you—"

"Lock it, or I'll be on you." He couldn't get any more clear than that. Or maybe, he could. *I'll be in you.*

Her eyes widened. She yanked a keycard out of her pocket and swiped it over the electronic lock. The lock engaged and bolted.

She stared at him. The bars of Cell A were thick, reinforced, and supposedly designed to keep even the strongest of paranormals inside.

There was a cot to the left of Duncan. A toilet. A sink.

She wrapped her hands around the bars. "Duncan, I'm so sorry this happened to you."

He stiffened. "I don't need your pity." Was the woman missing the whole bit where he was close to ripping her clothes off? "You need to get away from me. Stay away. Get another doctor to—"

"There is no other doctor here. Just me. You know that."

But she usually had an assistant who came in. At least during the days. The man who actually took the blood from the other werewolves.

Wait, before, Pate had said...*"It's the reason I wanted you away from the other wolves."*

What was the reason?

But the heat inside of his body started to build even more. It felt like he was being ripped apart by that fire.

Like...like the wolf was coming out.

"*Get away.*"

She let go of the bars, and her fingers skimmed over the remote on her belt. "Maybe I should adjust the silver intensity."

"It's not the fucking silver! It's you!" And, in an instant, he lost control. He leapt across the cell. Freaking *leapt* and was in front of her in less than a second's time. "I can smell you. I can taste you. And I want to fuck you." As if she'd missed that part before when he'd been driving his tongue into her mouth. "So you need to walk away. Walk away now. *Run* away. I don't know how strong this thing is inside of me, and if something should happen, if I got out of this cell..."

*Don't want to hurt her. Don't ever want to hurt her.*

"You need to be away from me," he finished.

Her gaze held his. Then she gave a slow nod and backed away from the cell.

He sucked in a deep breath. Dammit, he still *tasted* her.

Holly turned away. Her dark hair brushed over her white lab coat. She took two steps, then paused. "I wasn't saying no."

He didn't know what in the hell she was talking about.

Holly glanced over her shoulder. "I was kissing you back. And I bet I left more marks on you than you left on me."

His jaw wanted to drop.

"You told me what you wanted."

*I want to fuck you.*

"Maybe next time, you'll ask what I want." One dark brow climbed and she smiled. Wait, smiled? "Could be that it's the same thing you want."

It felt like she'd just punched him in the chest.

"Get some rest," she told him with a small nod. "The change is going to keep pumping through your body. It'll drain your energy. So just...rest, okay?"

Then she was heading down the hallway.

Leaving him alone in the cell—in the cage.

Leaving him with her scent still around him.

And leaving him with a wolf howling within him.

\*\*\*

It was the snarls that woke her. Holly jumped when the sounds pierced her consciousness. Her eyes flew open, and she realized that she was half-sprawled over her desk. She'd been waiting for the results of the screen on Duncan's blood, and she'd fallen asleep.

The snarls came again.

She jumped to her feet.

The clock on the desk said it was nearing 6 a.m. A fast glance toward her blinds didn't reveal the trickling light from dawn, not yet, but the fact that she'd fallen asleep told her that sunrise must be getting close.

Holly hurried toward the swinging doors of the med unit. With every step that she took, she heard—

*Snarls and growls.*

The sounds were getting louder. And she could hear yells. Screams? The cries weren't coming from Duncan's cell, but from the containment area on the opposite side of the base. She grabbed for her master remote, one that she kept as a precaution in case any of the wolves ever got loose.

*I do believe in having a Plan B.*

She ran toward those growls and screams.

When she shoved open the doors that led to the main containment area, the scent of blood hit her. Blood and—beast. Because wolves were there, wolves *not* in any cells. These weren't wolves that they had captured. She knew because there were no silver collars on the giant, snarling beasts. She counted four fully shifted wolves running near the cells, wolves that were attacking the guards who'd been stationed at the main containment area.

*Not just attacking them...*The guards were dead. Their screams had stopped.

How had the wolves gotten inside? How had they even found the base? The place was supposed to be secure, with guards on the exterior of the perimeter and—

The wolves were closing in on her.

Holly froze.

The remote wasn't going to do her any good. The three collared werewolves were still in their cages. They weren't moving at all. Just watching the carnage, still in human form.

Silver didn't bind the beasts coming toward her.

"Don't try to run," this came from the man in the first cell. His light green eyes locked on her. "They like it when prey runs."

So she was just supposed to stand there and let them eat her? Hell, no. She stumbled back a few steps—then slammed her hand on the alarm. The guards hadn't been given the chance to ring that alarm. Backup hadn't come for them.

*Please, let that backup come in time for me.*

The sound was high and shrill and designed to have the extra benefit of including multiple frequencies when it was activated. The techs had created the alarm after they'd studied canines for months. Humans couldn't hear the part of the alarm that would send a werewolf to his knees.

The Para Unit had wanted to be able to fight back against the beasts.

The wolves started to howl and snarl. One ran blindly forward and shoved his head into the wall.

They were distracted. Hurting. The alarm was driving them crazy—just as it was supposed to do.

"Don't!" The sharp order came from the green-eyed man. Saul. A werewolf who'd ripped the throats out of six homeless men in Seattle. "Don't run!" Saul said again. His face tightened with pain as he slammed his hands over his ears. Her frantic gaze locked on him. He was sagging to the ground as the alarm echoed through the facility. "They'll...kill you..."

No, they wouldn't. Not then. She'd get out. Seal the room up and—

"And...I...want to do that..." Saul's hands pulled from his ears. His fingers wrapped around the bars. "I want that sw-sweet blood..."

The bastard was saying he wanted to kill her? She yanked out the remote. Found the frequency for his collar and punched in the code to amp up his silver concentration.

He hit the floor, and she started to run.

Only she hadn't seen the fifth werewolf. The one who was blocking the exit. And coming at her even as he howled in pain.

***

Duncan heard her scream.

The alarm was shrieking, pain throbbed through his head, and Duncan heard Holly scream.

He didn't even know how he knew the high, desperate cry belonged to Holly, but...

*I fucking do.*

"Holly!" Duncan yelled as he grabbed at the silver bars. The silver burned his hands, but he didn't let go. He jerked, yanked. Nothing. The bars didn't so much as bend. "*Holly!*"

He only heard the continuing shriek of the alarm. He strained, trying to make out anything else, and...was that a growl? A snarl?

*Werewolves.*

Where the hell were the other agents?

Holly was in trouble. Holly could be hurt.

His claws were out. His lengthening canines stretching in his mouth. His fingers curled tightly around the bars, and he yanked once more and—

*Blood.*

He could smell blood, fresh blood.

Her blood.

*"Holly!"* He roared her name, and the cell bar snapped in his hand. One bar. Another. Another. Then he was breaking out of that cell, ripping away anything in his path. His muscles were stretching, aching, as he ran toward that scent.

But then...something happened to him. The fire that he'd felt in his body ignited into an inferno. Duncan fell to the floor, convulsing. Fur burst along his skin. His bones snapped. His muscles contorted.

He couldn't speak, not any longer. He could only growl and howl as the transformation swept over him. Brutal, excruciating, but lasting only for a matter of seconds. Then he was on his feet. All four of them. Running toward the blood because the scent was even stronger now.

He wasn't a man.

He was the beast.

And he was...hungry.

# CHAPTER THREE

The big, gray wolf had slashed Holly's arm. Her blood dripped on the floor as she edged back away from him. She had managed to retrieve a gun from one of the fallen guards—a gun he'd never had the chance to use—and she lifted the weapon now. The bullets would be silver. They'd better be. And she was about to fire a bullet right into that werewolf's head.

The door flew open behind the gray wolf and *another* wolf—this one even bigger, but with thick black fur and some damn huge teeth—came flying into the room.

Her gun swung toward the new threat because...yes, that wolf was focusing on her. Coming right toward her. Her hand tightened on the gun.

*I know those eyes.*

The black wolf had bright blue eyes. Blue eyes that were streaked with gold. Duncan's gaze.

She lowered her gun.

The gray wolf leapt at her.

She jumped back, barely avoiding another swipe from those powerful claws.

A howl of fury seemed to shake the room. Duncan's howl.

Then the black wolf slammed his body into the other beast. The gray wolf went down and Duncan—she turned away just as his teeth sank into the gray wolf's neck.

"Alpha..." The stark whisper came from Saul.

Her head jerked toward him. He was still clinging to the bars. Smiling, ignoring the shriek of the alarm and the smoke that drifted up from his clinging fingertips. "We can...smell him...others will want to fight...to see if they can take down...an alpha..."

"No one's taking him down," Holly snapped, but then she glanced back at Duncan.

The other wolves were up and circling Duncan. Going in to attack while he was fighting the gray wolf. They thought they'd gang up on Duncan?

Not on her watch.

"Get away from him!" Holly yelled and fired her gun. One bullet hit a white wolf in the flank. The wolf yelped.

She aimed again.

The doors burst open. Armed agents spilled into the room. About freaking time.

The wolves turned on this new threat. With their fangs bared, they lunged toward the agents. The agents began to fire at them.

To fire at Duncan? They wouldn't realize that Duncan was in wolf form. They'd think he was an attacker. They'd kill him, too.

"*No!*" Holly ran to Duncan and wrapped her arms around him. "Don't shoot! He's one of ours."

"Is he?" Came Saul's mocking voice.

She held Duncan tighter. His fur was soft against her skin and his sharp teeth were *way* too close to her neck. But she didn't back away from him. He needed her.

Howls and growls and the thunder of gunfire shook the room. When Duncan's body tensed, as if he'd spring to join the fight, her arms just held him tighter. "Don't," she whispered. "You'll just get shot, and I won't let you die like this." Shot down as a beast. That wasn't the end that waited for Duncan.

Then the gunfire stopped. The growls died away. She lifted her head and searched the area with a quick gaze.

Saul was laughing. "They'll...keep coming..."

Pate ran toward her. "Holly? Holly, are you all right?"

She nodded, but she didn't let go of Duncan.

"They'll keep coming...for him...already one alpha in this town," Saul said, voice deepening. "Already *one*."

What? Like one werewolf was going to dominate everything? The werewolves in this city needed to realize there was room for two alphas. Because Duncan wasn't dying.

Pate reached for her arm. Duncan lunged at him, snapping with his fangs.

"Easy." Pate put his hands up. He could have just shot Duncan, so she appreciated his restraint. One blond brow rose as Pate darted a glance at Holly. "I'm guessing that's our guy in there?"

Somewhere in the beast, yes, but she just didn't know how much of the man remained at that moment. Her fingers slid around his neck.

The collar was designed to automatically contract or expand to match a werewolf's transformation. A rather clever bit of technology that Pate was particularly proud of—since he'd designed it himself.

"Can you control him?" Pate asked.

She didn't want to use her remote to increase the silver levels hitting him. It just didn't seem right to hurt him when he'd come racing to her rescue. Holly wasn't exactly sure *how* he'd managed the escape from his cell, but she was grateful to him. So, instead of using the remote, her fingers stroked his fur. "Duncan?"

His head turned. His eyes—wild, shining so brightly—met hers.

"Can you shift back?" Holly whispered. "The agents are here. I'm safe now. Can you—can you shift?"

"You're not safe!" Saul yelled. He was getting on her nerves. The alarm had stopped shrieking, and he had gotten stronger. "That wolf...*he's* your biggest threat. You think I'm bad?" He laughed. "Wait until you see what an alpha can do to you."

At that, the black wolf pulled away from Holly. Rushed toward Saul's cage.

And growled.

Saul growled back.

Then Saul's eyelids flickered and he...lowered his head? Holly sucked in a gasp of surprise as Saul dropped to his knees in front of Duncan.

Wolf dynamics. They were scaring the crap out of her.

She glanced around the room once more. Saw the bodies. The dead werewolves were shifting back to human form. One woman. Four men.

Pate eased closer to Holly as the other agents went to check on the guards. Checking would do no good. They were dead. "You're bleeding." Pate's voice was tight. He didn't touch her. Probably because he was afraid of Duncan's reaction. She was a little afraid of it, too. "Did you get bitten?"

Holly shook her head. "It's just a scratch." From some very big claws. Her head turned. She met his gaze. "They attacked just after dawn." If they'd come sooner, she would have been able to fight back more.

He nodded, immediately understanding what she couldn't say with so many others close by.

"How did they get in?" Holly whispered. The facility *should* have been secure. "The guards outside—"

"Are dead." Flat, but emotion blazed in his eyes. "Slaughtered. These wolves came here because...fuck, I think they tracked *him*." The him in question...well, Pate was staring at Duncan.

Duncan's head turned toward them. She knew he'd heard what Pate had just said. With his enhanced werewolf hearing, Duncan could probably hear a pin dropping to the floor.

But why would the werewolves come for Duncan? Why—

Saul was still smiling.

Her eyes narrowed on him. She marched toward him, aware of throbbing in her arm from the werewolf attack. "Tell us what's happening here," she demanded. Because the guards inside were dead. The ones outside were dead. And the whole mess was nothing more than a *bloodbath*.

Saul kept grinning. She felt like giving the jerk something to grin about. *If it wasn't dawn...*

And then...Duncan let out a low howl. He tossed his head back and started to shift. The sound of the transformation was horrible. Muscles seemed to rip and tear. Bones broke. Snapped back together. His body contorted, and she had to lock down every muscle in her body so that she wouldn't run to him and try to help.

Because there was no help that she could give, and if she got too close during the shift, Holly knew he might attack her. Wolves lost control of their bodies during the shift. Their arms flew out, their legs kicked. She didn't want to chance another swipe from a werewolf's claws.

Then he was on the floor. Naked. Sprawled face-down. The muscles of his broad back were so strong, but trembling, and his ass—

*Wow.*

Great ass, and it was a very bad time for her to be noticing it.

Duncan pushed up to his feet. Pate tossed him a pair of sweats that he'd just pulled from a nearby storage locker. Duncan caught them, yanked them on, and had to put a hand on the cell's bar to steady himself.

When his fingers began to smoke, he lifted that hand away.

She couldn't stay back any longer. Holly took a step toward him.

But Duncan shook his head. "Don't."

The one, clipped word felt like a slap in the face.

Then Duncan moved in a lightning-fast lunge. His hand shot through the side of the cage, sliding right between the bars. His fingers wrapped around Saul's neck, and he jerked werewolf forward. Saul's head slammed into the bars. Smoke rose.

"She wants to know..." Duncan said, voice so rough and deep, "what the hell is happening here. Why did those wolves attack?"

Saul couldn't speak, mostly because Duncan seemed to be choking him. Saul's face had turned a dark shade of purple.

"Uh, you need to ease that grip," Pate muttered as he came closer to Duncan. "You know the dead can't talk."

That wasn't entirely true. *Sometimes they can.*

Holly fisted her hands and refused to reach out again to Duncan. He'd already shot her down once in front of Pate and the others.

Duncan's grip on the werewolf eased. Saul sucked in a deep breath. Another.

Then he started talking. "They can...smell you."

A faint furrow appeared between Duncan's brows.

"Alpha scent," Holly whispered, understanding.

Pate gave a barely perceptible nod.

"When you changed, they *knew*..." Saul's breath wheezed out. He still wasn't free of Duncan's grip, but at least he was getting oxygen now. "But a human doesn't just get to be...top dog...you have to...fight for it..."

"I don't want to be the damn top dog," Duncan snapped, "I don't want—"

"Not about what *you* want. About what the...beast inside wants." Saul's gaze darted to Holly. "He's gonna...take what he wants."

The words seemed like a threat.

Saul's gaze returned to Duncan. "You'll have to fight...prove your worth. Then you can lead the pack."

"Screw that." Duncan released him and moved back a few feet. "I'm not interested in the pack. I don't want—"

"Then you're dead." Saul straightened his shoulders, seemed to gather his strength. "You fight and win, you lead...or you die." Saul tilted his head as he studied Duncan. "This town can't take two alphas."

"Who's the other alpha?" Holly demanded. They were still learning about werewolf dynamics, but if the dead werewolves had been sent to attack Duncan, then it sure stood to reason that the other alpha had been the one to send them out on the hunt.

But Saul just smirked at her. "Don't worry, you'll be finding out, sweets, soon enough."

Yes, those words were definitely a threat.

"And *you'll* be getting sliced open," Duncan said as he lifted his claws. "Soon damn enough if you don't tell me where the other alpha is."

"I can help you," Saul offered as he paled. He held up his hands, palms out. The gesture probably would have looked more innocent if he hadn't been sporting two-inch-long claws on his fingertips.

"Yeah, you can," Duncan agreed. The sweats hung low on his hips. "Tell me where to find the alpha. Tell me who the bastard is."

Saul licked his lips. "Get me out of here. Give me my freedom. Then we'll talk."

Pate laughed, drawing Saul's attention. "Are you kidding me? You carved up humans! Six of them. I'm pretty sure you even *ate* one of the poor bastards. You aren't getting out of here. You're going to Purgatory, and you're not getting out."

*Purgatory.*

The name of the only prison for paranormals that existed. Until recently, the only way to stop a paranormal had been to kill him. Or her. But now...even though most humans didn't even know about the existence of the paranormal creatures, Uncle Sam wanted them treated more humanely.

So Purgatory had been created. Modeled after Alcatraz, the prison was supposed to be inescapable. Located on a tiny island off the coast of Washington, the walls had been made out of a special metal formulated by the government. An unbreakable metal with silver components.

Inside, all of the cells were secured with silver bars. The guards used weapons that contained either wooden bullets—when they were in the vampire wards—or silver bullets—when they were guarding the werewolves.

Purgatory had been in operation for over a year, and, so far, the prison seemed to be doing its job—keeping the most dangerous of the paranormals locked up and away from humans.

The only prison of its kind in the world, Purgatory would succeed or...it would fail, horribly.

Personally, the idea of having all of the most dangerous paranormals in one small place...um, yeah, that idea terrified Holly. But no one had listened to her when she went before the small committee in D.C. and told them it was a *very* bad idea.

She was just the MD who'd been brought into the Seattle Para Unit because of her connection to Pate. The suits wanted her reports, not her take on Armageddon.

"You aren't getting out," Duncan said to Saul, shaking his head.

Saul's jaw hardened. "You think you're so different from me?"

The dead guards had been taken away, but the scent of blood lingered in the air. Holly swallowed a few times as her head began to throb. She realized that she'd lost more blood from her attack than she'd initially realized.

Too much blood. Her kind had a tendency to bleed too freely when injured.

"They'll have *you* in a cage soon!" Saul threw at Duncan.

Holly barely controlled a wince at the guy's shriek because the truth was that actually, they'd already put him in a cage.

But Duncan had somehow gotten out, and he'd rushed in to help her.

"Don't you get it?" Saul's lengthening teeth snapped together. "It's us against them. You're not human anymore. You're better." He spat toward Pate.

*Uh, oh.* The guy shouldn't try to piss off Pate.

Pate held out his hand to Holly.

She knew he wanted the remote. She also knew this part wasn't going to be pretty. "Pate..."

His hand waited. No expression crossed his face.

"Tell us where the alpha is," Pate said softly as he kept his gaze on Saul, "or you're going to find yourself in a great deal of pain soon."

Sometimes, it was hard for her to remember Pate the way he'd been...before. Before he'd learned about the paranormals out in the world. Before he'd become so single-minded and focused on the Para Unit's mission. Pate was determined to take the killers off the streets—the *paranormal* killers.

She wondered, secretly because she could never tell him, just how far would Pate be willing to go in order to stop the monsters that he hunted? Just what would he do?

*Risk his own men? Set them up so that they could be exposed, could be transformed?*

*Would he risk his own sister?*

Saul's hands rose to the collar that circled around his throat. "Gonna punch it up? Gonna make me scream?"

"Yes," Pate said with a nod. "I will. If it means I can keep my men alive, I'll do anything." His gaze cut to Holly. "The remote." Impatience crackled in his words.

Locking her jaw, she gave it to him, but her stare met Saul's. "There's no need for this. Just tell us where to find the other alpha. *Tell us.*" *So you don't burn.*

His nostrils flared. "All that sweet smelling blood...do you taste like dessert? I bet you do—"

Duncan shoved his hand through the bars again, but this time, Saul leapt back. "I'm dead if I tell you! So use the remote." He pointed at Pate. "Blast me with the silver. I don't care! If I talk, *I die.*"

It was obvious to Holly that he feared the alpha out in the city far more than he feared any pain they could give to him.

Pate glanced down at the remote. Then Pate looked back up at her. "Go outside, Holly. Maybe I was wrong about all of the guards out there. If any of them survived, they'll need you."

Right. Right. She should have thought—

She turned away, rushing for the door.

"Good-bye, Holly." Duncan's voice. Rumbling.

She risked a quick glance back over shoulder. His gaze was on hers. And he looked so...sad.

"I'll be back," she whispered.

His lips twisted into what could have been a smile. But wasn't. Too rough. Too hard.

Then she was running out of that containment area. Hurrying for her office, and she *knew* that Pate had just wanted to get rid of her. He hadn't wanted her to hear what was coming. She could have argued, could have stayed, but if some of the guards were still alive, she had to help them.

And she had to leave Duncan behind.

*** 

Pate took Duncan into his office. Duncan had been in Pate's office before, plenty of times, but this was the only time that he'd ever felt like he was a suspect.

Pate locked the door behind him. "We don't have a lot of options here."

What was with the "we" business? The last time Duncan had checked, Pate was still human.

He was the one sprouting fur and running on all fours.

"The moon rises in a few days. If your wolf is taking over, it'll happen then."

A few days wasn't exactly much of a countdown. Duncan turned his head, and his gaze raked suspiciously over the guy who'd been his boss since he'd joined the unit. "Did you know?"

Pate's blond brows rose. "Know that we'd get attacked this morning? That my men would be slaughtered? Hell, no, I didn't—"

"Did you know that I could change into a werewolf?" Because when he'd joined the team, Holly had been one of the first people he'd seen. She'd drawn his blood and performed a slate of tests on him. Procedure, or at least that was what Pate had told him.

But now he wasn't so sure if it had just been pure procedure. Had Pate been screening the recruits? Checking to see if any of them had DNA that would make them susceptible to a werewolf's bite? Had he looked to see who could possibly change? "Did you know?" Duncan gritted again because the tight knot in his stomach wasn't easing up.

"I knew." Quiet.

Duncan's eyes narrowed. He hadn't expected Pate to confess to the truth so easily. Duncan crossed his arms over his bare chest and waited to hear the rest.

Only Pate didn't speak.

Jaw locking, Duncan asked, "Did you *want* me to become a werewolf?" That wasn't the question he wanted to ask. He wanted to know...*Did you set me up to become a monster?*

He was starting to think his boss just might be cold-blooded enough to have done so.

"I wanted you to be an agent on my team. I wanted you to do your job and take out the monsters that were preying on humans." Pate stalked toward him. "Every member of my team goes through testing because we have to be prepared for any eventuality. If there's a chance that a team member will turn, I have to be ready for that situation."

"You didn't tell *me*. No one bothered to share any test results with me. Don't you think I had a right to know?"

"And if you *had* known?" Pate threw right back as he squared off against Duncan. "Would you have turned down the job? Not gone out and hunted because you were afraid of the risk? Dammit, man, you'd already had run-ins with werewolves just working as a Seattle detective. You could have been bitten at any time. It wasn't the unit's fault that you changed."

*It wasn't mine.*

Those were the words that Pate didn't say, but they still seemed to hang in the air.

"And if I go fucking crazy?" Duncan wanted to know, because, yeah, that was a real possibility. One that no one could sugarcoat for him. Some newly transformed wolves couldn't handle the beast within them and they went mad. "When that moon rises and my beast takes over, what then?" The full moon would be the most dangerous time. The telling time. If the beast was going to be too strong for the man in him to control, then madness could take him then.

But Pate was shaking his head. "I've already got it figured out for you."

Right. He just bet the boss did.

"You just need an anchor," Pate said. "Something to hold you in check."

Duncan laughed. "Let me guess...Holly's got a little drug for that?" He knew that she and Pate had been the ones to design the silver collars, an invention that the Powers-That-Be in the FBI loved. Pate did the gadgetry, and Holly did the science. Together, they were supposed to be unbeatable.

Good for them.

"Holly *may* have something for you, yes," Pate said softly as a furrow appeared between his brows.

The faintest flicker of hope lit within Duncan. "Don't bullshit me." If there was a chance that he wouldn't go crazy, that he wouldn't turn on the humans...

*Then I don't have to die.* Because he'd been ready to meet death if it meant he'd spare innocent lives.

Pate's stare was steady. "If I'd thought there was no hope for you, I would have let Elias put his gun to your head."

Fair enough. The hope kept growing.

"Like I said, Holly *may* be able to help you. She's a woman with surprising resources."

Duncan's eyes narrowed. He wasn't the only agent there who'd wondered about the rather...close...relationship between Pate and Holly. What was going on with those two?

Were they involved?

*They'd better not be.*

"But before we get to the moonrise," Pate continued, seemingly oblivious to Duncan's glare, "we have to deal with the other alpha. I don't think he's just going to let you live peacefully until then."

Highly doubtful, and Duncan didn't want more human guards getting caught in the battle. Unfortunately, Saul and the other wolves in containment weren't talking. They were too afraid of the alpha. They feared him more than they feared death by silver.

Duncan exhaled slowly and glanced down at his hands. The claws were gone, for the moment. He hated that they seemed to spring out on their own. As soon as he got angry—bam, there they were.

Pate revealed, "Our intel indicates that he moved into town about eight months ago."

"Then the murders kicked up," Duncan muttered. The wolves had begun to kill, not caring if they drew attention from the humans.

"We know the guy is in his mid-thirties. He blew into town, seemingly with no past, and the guy likes to stay hidden."

When you had a pack eager to obey you, it was easy enough to hide behind them.

Pate's eyes narrowed. "I think it's past time we find the bastard's hiding place. We've got the perfect bait back in that containment area. Bait that can lead you right to the alpha. We can take him out, and, without him to follow, the wolves in this city will splinter."

Duncan rocked forward onto the balls of his feet. "Bait?"

"Saul." Pate shook his head. "I don't want to let him go—"

"You *said* you wouldn't—"

"But if we track the jerk, keep him monitored twenty-four, seven, we can follow him back to the alpha."

Duncan's heart started to pound faster. "And what will you do if he gets away from your monitoring, huh? He's a werewolf, it's not exactly easy to track his kind."

"It is if another werewolf is doing the hunting."

They stared at each other.

"You want *me* to follow Saul."

Pate nodded. "Not only that, I want you to be the one to get him out of his cage."

What the hell? "Did you hit your head in the attack? Take a shot? Something?" Because this plan was shit.

Pate's smile was cold. "In that containment room, I made myself his enemy."

"I was the one choking the bastard." Because of the way Saul had looked at Holly. As if the werewolf could already taste her. *No one else gets near her.*

The wolf inside was still pissed. Or maybe the man was. Right then, it was hard to tell the difference between them.

"I told Saul that I wouldn't make a deal with him." Pate walked around behind his desk and sat in the leather chair. He flattened his hands on the desk's scarred surface. "And I won't make a deal, but you will. One wolf to another."

He didn't like where this was going. "You're just gonna let me open his cage?"

"Um..." A small nod. "And you need to do it now, while the other agents are all distracted by the recent attack. It will look more real that way. It has to look real to Saul. He needs to believe that you're working with him. If he believes you, if he trusts you...then Saul might even wind up siding with you and *helping* you to take out the alpha."

There seemed to be a whole lot of *ifs* involved in the equation, but they didn't exactly seem to have a whole lot of options. Either they could wait for the alpha to attack again or Duncan could launch his own attack first.

"Get his trust," Pate directed. "Use him. Take out the alpha."

Easier said than done.

"Don't worry about human casualties. The collar that Saul wears will transmit his location to us every minute. He won't get free."

Pate was way too confident. "It's not the getting free part that worries me. It's the whole slicing the throats of humans part." Like Saul had already done, six times before. He'd gone after the homeless deliberately because the werewolf had a taste for the helpless and weak.

"Your job is to make sure he doesn't hurt anyone, *Agent* McGuire. Consider yourself Saul's federal guard, if that makes you feel better."

Was Pate crazy? "I'm the one we need to watch! I need a guard!" He lifted his hands. With his increased heartbeat and the tension that was eating away at him, sure enough, the claws were pushing out again. "Screw Saul. He's got years of control—"

"No, he obviously doesn't, or he wouldn't be killing."

"I could be the one to go bad. *I* could start killing."

"And that's why you're wearing a collar, too."

He barely felt the weight of the silver around his neck. Probably because Holly had set it for the lightest possible intensity level. She hadn't wanted to hurt him.

And he...

*I want her.*

Duncan cleared his throat. He had to stay away from her. When he was near Holly, he just thought about fucking.

Or killing anyone who wanted to hurt her.

The beast was way too unstable when she was near.

Pate held up the remote he'd taken from Holly. "There are several master remotes at this facility. And the silver can't just be amped up...the setting can be switched to kill mode."

So Duncan had always suspected.

"You go rogue, you start attacking humans, don't worry, I'll take you out myself."

Good to know.

"Now time is running out." The lines near Pate's eyes deepened. "If you're not in for this plan, then—"

"You think I'm stable enough to handle this?" A question that had to be asked. "Another shift could come. I can't—I can't stop the shift." He'd been so angry before when he'd been in his cell and he'd heard Holly's screams. Enraged and afraid for Holly. The shift had swept over him, and there'd been nothing he could do to stop it.

But then, he hadn't been sure that he wanted to stop it then. He'd wanted to attack whoever—whatever—had been hurting her.

"We wanted you to stay the night at the facility so that Holly could do her tests." One brow rose even as Pate's gaze dropped to his neck. "So you'd be collared."

*And you'd have your automatic kill switch?*

"But you aren't a prisoner here. You're a federal agent. A man who has always done his job and protected the innocent. You can walk out of this building anytime you want." A pause. "Though I'd prefer for you to leave in the next five minutes...with Saul."

Taking Saul anywhere was going to be a risk. "I want a master remote."

Pate immediately tossed it to him. "Done. Saul's code is 7943."

"And my code?"

Pate smiled.

Right.

"I know it. Holly knows it. So I'd say we're covered on that end," Pate told him.

No, Pate was covered.

"Are you going to tell the others what I'm doing?" Duncan asked. He'd rather prefer not to get shot down by his own team members.

Pate nodded. "*After* you're gone, they'll all know."

"Not before?"

"We need to make it look real," a soft murmur.

So it looked like he was going to do this. All right. Fine. He motioned toward himself. "I think I'll need more clothes."

"Back up gear and clothing are waiting outside. Go in the hall, then take the fourth door on your right."

Duncan turned away.

"Ah...just one more thing, McGuire."

Wasn't there always one more thing with Pate?

"I've noticed that you seem to be reacting a bit...intently to Holly."

Understatement of the century.

"You're too dangerous to be around a woman right now in any sort of sexual capacity." Pate's voice had hardened. "So I'm giving you an order. Stay away from her."

The wolf growled. The sound hung in the air.

"I'm still your director here." Pate's chair squeaked and Duncan knew the guy had shot to his feet. "You will listen to what I say and—"

Duncan glanced back over his shoulder. Pate's eyes widened as he gazed at Duncan's face. *What does he see there?* "Staying away from her may not be an option." Not when the moon rose. He was very much afraid that when the moon rose, the wolf would go straight to her. "You work on keeping *her* away from *me*. Send her away from this place. Get her out of the town. Do whatever you need to do."

"Why? Why her?"

"Because the beast knows I want her." *I can still taste her.* "And he wants her too."

Then Duncan yanked open the door and hurried down the hallway. He had a serial killing werewolf waiting for him. One that needed to get broken out of his cell.

\*\*\*

The guards outside were dead. So much blood. Everywhere. The attack from the werewolves had been brutal.

The scent of that blood...it was so strong.

Feeling light-headed, Holly stumbled back inside. Her shaking body told her that she'd gone too long without her dose. She knew how dangerous her condition was, and she should have been paying more attention to the passage of time.

But the little matter of the attacking werewolves had distracted her.

She hurried into the med unit, then made her way into the section she'd designated for her lab. She just needed one dose to get her through the next twelve hours, and—

"She smells so sweet."

The rasping voice froze Holly in her tracks. It was a familiar voice. Saul's voice.

"Why does she smell that way?" Saul asked.

Then a hand was curving over her shoulder. A hand with long, thick claws. Saul's hand. Holly opened her mouth to scream.

But the cry never left her lips. Because suddenly Duncan was there, and he put *his* hand over her mouth, choking back the cry.

*Duncan?* No, no, he wouldn't hurt her. He'd helped her before.

"You shouldn't be in here now," Duncan whispered. His lips brushed over her cheek and a shiver shuddered through her body. "You were supposed to be outside. Helping the guards."

There were no guards to help. But she would have still been out there, securing the bodies, if she hadn't gone too long without her dose. She'd been afraid to go any longer without it.

Her hand slid into the pocket of her lab coat.

"She's going for the remote!" Saul's fierce warning as his hand jerked from her shoulder and grabbed hold of her wrist. His grip was brutal as he twisted her hand, and the bones snapped.

She was staring straight into Duncan's eyes when her wrist broke. His stare was blue, with streaks of gold, but as she cried out in pain, the gold seemed to explode in his gaze. He released her instantly, and he grabbed Saul—then threw the man across the room. Saul crashed onto the operating table. *"You don't hurt her!"* Duncan roared.

Holly stumbled back. Her wrist throbbed and...the bones were facing the wrong way. She grabbed her wrist with her left hand, and yanked the bones back into place. A tight, high moan escaped her as the pain shot through her again.

"Holly..." Duncan growled her name.

Fumbling, her left hand managed to grab the remote.

"Stop her!" Saul yelled as he leapt back to his feet. "Stop her or every agent left in this building will come after us!"

Duncan caught her left wrist in his hand. His grip was gentle but strong. "I can't let you stop us."

"Us?" Holly whispered and shook her head. "There is no 'us', Duncan. There's you. And then there's a killer." Nausea rolled in her stomach. *The dose.* She needed it so badly. The pain she felt just made her all the more desperate to have it.

Saul ran toward them.

Before he could reach for Holly, Duncan swung out at him. This time, Saul slammed back and crashed into a cabinet. Bottles fell. Shattered. Bags of blood hit the floor, and Saul's claws cut right through them as he scrambled back to his feet.

Holly tried to lurch forward.

Duncan snatched the remote from her. He shattered it in his hands. Then he pulled her against him. "I'm sorry." He barely breathed the words into her ear.

"Let me go!" He didn't understand what was happening. His wolf must be trying to take over, just as he'd feared and—

"You can't stop us." He lifted her up. Carried her to the table on the right.

She struggled against him, fighting with all of her strength, but she was no match for him. Not then. Not with the sun up and her body desperate for a dosage. And certainly not with his new enhanced strength pulsing through his body.

He strapped her down. Her legs first. Then her stomach. Her chest. Her left arm. Her right— her right hand he lifted to his mouth, and he pressed a kiss to her wrist. "I'm sorry," he said again.

Then he...left her there. Strapped to the table.

Just. Left. Her.

She opened her mouth to scream. What the hell had she been thinking? She should have been screaming the whole time! She'd just been stunned. Shocked.

Betrayed.

Now her scream ripped from her, only to be quieted into a muffled groan when Duncan tied a twisted cloth around her head—and put part of that cloth in her mouth.

"Oh, damn, but she looks good that way." Saul was coming back toward her.

Holly tensed. She could see his claws.

"Let's just slice her, a little bit..."

Duncan grabbed Saul's hand, keeping those claws away from Holly. "We're getting out of here." His shoulders lifted. Fell. "I want to run."

Saul smiled. "The beast. It wants out." He nodded quickly. "You were right to get me. I can help you. We can stick together. Fuckin' destroy anyone who comes after us." His gaze lingered on Holly. "Anyone."

Duncan wasn't looking at her.

He was just whirling away and running toward the room on the right. Toward the secret entrance and exit to the facility that only she and the other agents knew about. The guards on staff didn't even know about that room—agents only.

So much for security. That exit would take Duncan and Saul *past* all of the security. Past the guards who were now being extra vigilant. It would take them to freedom.

She shook her head.

But Duncan didn't see the movement.

He didn't see anything she did. Because he left her there. Tied. Gagged. With her wrist broken and her whole body aching.

She hadn't gotten her dose. She'd needed it but...

But it was gone. Destroyed by Saul. Smeared on the floor.

A tear leaked down her cheek. Duncan was gone.

And there was no way to stop him. His beast was coming out.

She pitied anyone who was in his path when Duncan's shift was complete.

# CHAPTER FOUR

The sonofabitch had broken Holly's wrist. Just snapped her delicate bones. Her face had bleached of color. Her pupils had dilated as her eyes showed the flash of agony she felt.

And Duncan had almost taken Saul's head.

"You did it!" Saul slapped Duncan on the shoulder. "Man, I thought it was a trick, but you got us the fuck out of there."

They were away from the facility. In the middle of nowhere. Pate had set up the containment compound far away from the busy city streets. Here, the wilderness stretched, and wild animals waited.

He should fit in perfectly with his animal.

*I still want to take Saul's head.*

"I did my part," Duncan said, fighting to keep his words steady. "I got us out of there. Now you— you take me to the alpha."

"So you can die?" Saul rocked back on his heels. "I've never seen anyone with a death wish like yours."

"So I can kill *him*." Duncan lifted his claws. "I'm alpha, and I'm staying alpha." Was that the right thing to say? He hoped it was. He needed

Saul to get his ass in gear and lead him to the alpha.

But Saul was laughing. "You just changed! There's no way that you're a match for him yet. You try to fight him, the guy will rip you in two." Saul shoved away from him. "Thanks for the free pass out, but this is where we part ways."

"The hell it is!" He heaved out a hard breath and grabbed Saul's arm. "Do you want to be the wolf that the Seattle pack goes after?"

"I will be if I take you to—"

"Because when I kick the alpha's ass and take over, I'll have every single one of those dogs looking for you. *You'll* be at the top of my list."

Saul's gaze slid away from his. "You won't take him out. No one has ever been able to defeat him."

"He hasn't faced me before."

Saul hesitated. "You...you think you can—"

Duncan's nostrils flared. A new scent had just come into the area. Sex and honey. *No*.

Saul's eyes widened, and Duncan knew he'd caught the scent, too. Then a twig snapped behind them.

Saul's lips peeled away from his teeth, and he started to launch toward Holly.

Duncan jerked Saul back even as he whirled to face Holly. "*Get back!*" He didn't know how she'd gotten out of those straps so quickly, but she'd just walked into hell.

Instead of running away, Holly lifted her left hand. In that hand she had—*sonofabitch*—another remote. Staring into his eyes, she aimed the remote at him. Duncan went down to his knees as pain shot from his neck all the way through his body.

Footsteps thundered as Saul raced away.

Holly lunged forward, obviously planning to stop Saul, too.

Duncan leapt for her. His body hit hers—*I'm sorry, I'm sorry, Holly*—and she cried out at the impact. They slammed into the earth, and the remote fell from her fingers.

He caught her hands, pinned them above her head, but tried to be as gentle as he could with her broken wrist. She was going to scream. He could see the intention right there on her face.

He kissed her, muffling the sound.

She bit him and drew blood from his bottom lip. He pressed his mouth harder against hers, growling, and she suddenly stiffened.

Had he hurt her? He wanted to lift his head, but was afraid she'd scream if he did.

Then he didn't have to worry about lifting his head because he was flying through the air. She'd just tossed him against a tree.

Sent him flying a good five freaking feet. How in the hell had the little doc done that?

Instantly, he leapt to his feet. Holly was also on her feet, and she stared at him with wide, horrified eyes.

Saul's footsteps were a quiet thud in the distance. The werewolf could sure move fast when he wanted to haul ass. He was running now, heading for safety.

A safety that Duncan suspected would take him to Seattle's ruling alpha.

Holly had her hand over her mouth. "Your blood..."

He stiffened. "Don't worry, you won't change. I'd have to be the one to bite *you* for that to happen."

She shook her head. Her eyes were so dark. Deep and dark, and he could stare into them forever.

Saul's footsteps were even softer now.

Duncan shook his head. "Don't follow me again." He had Saul's scent. Time to track the bastard back to the alpha's hiding spot.

"No, Duncan! Stop!"

He shook his head. "Get away from me." *You're safe when you're away from me.*

"I can help you!" Holly's lips were red. Her teeth...sharp? "Let me help you."

"Help yourself. Go back to Pate. Don't come near me again." He inhaled a deep breath. Caught more of her scent. His whole body tightened. "Because if I see you again, you won't walk away from me."

He didn't know how to make that any plainer.

This was her last chance to be free.

\*\*\*

"Holly!"

She flinched when Pate grabbed her hand. She'd heard him coming. No missing the frantic pounding of his footsteps, but she hadn't moved at his approach.

She could taste Duncan. "Stay away from me." Her voice came out far too flat. Funny, she was giving Pate pretty much the same warning that Duncan had given to her.

No, it wasn't funny. More like tragic. Her hands clenched into fists.

He instantly dropped his hold. "Look, it's not what you think, okay?" His voice was a whisper. "I can explain, but not out here. Come back inside with me."

She couldn't look away from the trees. Duncan had run through those trees just a few moments before. "I missed my dose."

Pate swore. "I saw the mess in your lab. There's a backup dose, don't worry. You'll be—"

"Duncan kissed me. I-I bit his lip." And she'd tasted his blood. Just one drop.

One drop shouldn't matter.

It did.

Pate began to back away from her. "How much time do I have?"

She was barely holding onto her control. "Not long enough." Her voice was soft now.

He started to run. Not after Duncan or Saul. But he was running away...from her.

Because her own monster was about to come out.

She could feel her teeth burning and stretching in her mouth. If she'd just gotten the dose, everything would have been fine. But she'd had that one drop of blood.

Fresh blood.

From a live source.

One. Single. Drop.

It was the first taste that was supposed to be the most tempting. She'd been warned of this. At the first taste of blood from a *live* source, the bloodlust would overwhelm her. She'd attack anyone near.

At the first taste...

She'd tried to be so careful. Getting her doses. Only taking blood from bags. Not directly from a person, never that...because you could taste emotions when you drank the blood from a live source.

That taste was addictive.

"I'm sorry," Holly whispered to Pate. He'd tried to help her. He'd been the one to give her access to the bags, but she'd slipped up.

One drop.

Her control splintered.

She spun around and sprang at Pate. He hadn't been able to make it to safety. He was too far from the facility. And he couldn't run nearly fast enough to get away from her.

She bared her fangs at him. The frantic pounding of his heartbeat filled her ears. The drumming sound pulled her closer. Closer.

She leapt for him. In the next second, she had her arms wrapped around him. She pushed up onto her toes and put her mouth on his throat.

"I'm sorry, Holly," he told her quietly. "I should have taken better care of you."

There was a gun right at her heart. She could feel the press of the cold metal through her shirt.

She should have known that Pate would be armed. He always was.

He pulled the trigger.

\*\*\*

"Holly."

She shook her head, content to stay in the darkness that surrounded her.

"Holly, I know it hurts, but just hold on. The dose is almost finished."

Pate. He sounded worried.

He should be worried. He'd shot her.

After she'd tried to kill him.

"That's it. You should have everything that you need." She felt a light tug on her arm, near her elbow. Then his fingers brushed back her hair. "I'm gonna dig the bullet out, and when I do, you'll be able to move again."

The bullet. Ah, yes, that would be why her chest hurt like a bitch.

And why she couldn't move so much as a single part of her body.

There was a surge of pressure on her chest and then...

The darkness vanished as her eyes opened. She sucked in a deep, shuddering breath.

Pate's arms tightened around her. "You just scared the shit out of me."

*My lab.* He'd carried her back inside. She was on the floor. Half-cradled in his arms.

The shame of what she'd done burned through her. "I went...for your throat."

He held her tighter. "You weren't yourself. You'd just gotten *werewolf* blood. You know the effect that it has on your kind."

She did. Werewolf blood was reportedly like a drug to *her* kind—giving them a burst of pleasure, of euphoria, that was rumored to be better than sex.

"The first time you get blood from a live source, and that source had to be a werewolf." He sounded disgusted. "Hell, there was no way at all you were maintaining control after that."

She had control now, though. Her gaze dropped to the floor beside her. Pate had given her a transfusion—a whole lot of blood. Well, that would explain the having-control bit.

"What you saw in the woods...it wasn't what you thought. I gave Duncan orders. He's going to keep Saul on a leash and use him so that we can find the alpha."

So Duncan hadn't been betraying the unit. Her lashes swept down even as relief rose within her.

"When I brought Duncan back here to you, I *never* thought you'd get his blood. Sis, I swear, I never did."

She heard the remorse in his voice, and Holly wanted to believe him.

But she couldn't. Not entirely. Because she knew him better than anyone else. He could be so manipulative.

If he thought he was helping in the battle against the monsters out there, would he risk her life?

*He'd risk everything.*

She pulled away from him. The wooden bullet—covered with her blood—was in his hand. "Did anyone see?" Holly whispered.

What she was—it was their secret. One they'd protected the entire time she'd been working in the unit.

He shook his head. "I carried you inside. No one saw anything."

Good. "What happens now?" She'd slipped up. Made the mistake that she'd always feared. Pate had been so confident that no one would ever learn about her. That she'd be safe, as long as she had access to the doses she needed. And in her own lab, a place guarded by a dozen agents, he'd promised that she'd have the security she wanted.

Only she wasn't safe anymore. Neither was he.

*I had Duncan's blood.*

"Nothing happens. We continue just as before."

Her jaw dropped. "You can't be serious! I almost killed you."

His fingers closed over the bullet. "And I did kill you."

Only she hadn't stayed dead. She couldn't. That was the way with her kind. As long as a wooden bullet was in her heart, her body would mimic death. Once the bullet was out...she came back to life, so to speak.

The real truth was that she'd died a year ago.

"Go home. Sleep. Wash away the blood." His words were clipped, and they were also no longer given in the softer tone of a brother, but rather in the more demanding snap of a boss. "Then you come back here tonight, and you carry on the same as before."

She rose to her feet. She was already stronger. Thanks to the dose.

*The dose...call it what it is...the blood.* Though often, the blood was combined with a special drug mix that was supposed to keep her urges in check. "We can't keep on like this." She was fighting her instincts. Trying to be something that she wasn't.

Human.

"We'll keep on until you find a cure."

There was no cure. He didn't get that. It wasn't that she was sick. She wasn't human anymore.

"Go home," Pate ordered again as a muscle jerked in his jaw. "Everything will be better soon."

Pate. So wrong. So lost.

He blamed himself for what she'd become.

Sometimes, late at night, she blamed him, too. That was her shame.

"If you can't come up with a cure, then I'll get another doctor in. You know I can pull any damn strings I want, and I heard that Forbes was in the area."

Jonathan Forbes. The name had her tensing. He was good with DNA. He was also a prick. And her ex-fiancé.

They'd split when she'd suddenly developed an appetite for blood. "Jonathan is more interested in slicing and dicing paranormals than he is in helping them." That had been one of the main reasons she ran from him.

She hadn't wanted to wind up as one of his experiments.

Silence. Then, "But he *can* do the job. There aren't a whole lot of doctors in the know when it comes to the paranormals."

No, there weren't.

Pate continued, "I'll make sure that he monitors Duncan."

While she—what? Hid in the shadows?

"I'm not telling you this as your brother. I'm giving you an order as the senior agent for this unit. You're to stay away from Duncan McGuire from now on."

Easier said than done. She could still taste him, and she was...craving him. "You sent him out there, all alone, to fight the Seattle alpha?"

"He *is* an alpha."

"What if he gets killed?" Didn't Pate get it? Duncan didn't want to be a werewolf. Maybe facing off against the other alpha was his way of making sure his death wish was granted.

*I won't let that happen.*

"We're tracking Duncan through the chip in his collar. If necessary, we can send backup to him." Pate shook his head. Narrowed his eyes on her. "Go home, Holly. Just...*go*. When you're back in control, then you can return to the lab later."

In control. Right. Because she always had to stay in control. Always had to be so careful.

Maybe she was tired of being careful. She stared at her brother. Saw all the secrets he carried in his eyes. He'd told her the unit was necessary. For the protection of the humans.

Only she wasn't human anymore.

Neither was Duncan.

And Pate was still using them both.

"Screw control," she told him as she turned and walked away. It wasn't about control. It was about helping a man who'd just lost everything.

Pate might be willing to sit back and watch the brutal battle unfold before him, but she wasn't going to do that.

One drop of Duncan's blood. Just one. That was all she'd gotten.

It was all she needed. She could *feel* Duncan now. Could sense him.

And could track him. She didn't need the collar to give her his location. Now, with his blood, she'd be able to find him anywhere, anytime.

If he was facing off against the wolves, she'd make sure he had backup.

The supernatural kind.

\*\*\*

Pate didn't move so much as a muscle as his stepsister walked away. Holly was so small and deceptively delicate.

The perfect killing machine.

He hadn't wanted this life for her, but...but there was no going back.

His nightmares wouldn't stop. He could still see her attack, over and over again in his head like a broken movie reel that wouldn't stop playing.

But now...Holly was finally becoming stronger. Not the broken doll, the one who hid in the lab because she didn't want to face the world outside.

She'd tasted Duncan's blood. *Gone for my throat.*

Her killer instincts were showing.

The doors swung closed behind her.

And Pate finally let his smile sweep over his face.

***

Holly went to her home first, mostly because she had a bullet hole in her shirt and the fabric was covered with blood. She jumped into the shower and let the water slide over her skin. She'd get clean, then she'd find Duncan.

He wouldn't die before she washed the blood away. At least, she hoped he didn't and—

Her alarm was beeping. A high-pitched whine that she still barely heard over the roar of her shower. Frowning, she hurriedly turned off the water until only a *drip-drip-drip* remained.

The whine was clear now. Clear and plenty loud.

Her gaze tracked to the left. She couldn't see anything through the steamed-up glass door of her shower. But that alarm had been set off by something.

Someone.

She heard a creak. Very soft. Too close. The creak had come from her bedroom.

Fingers trembling, she pushed open the shower door and grabbed for her towel.

"Hello, sweets." A drawling, dark voice.

Her head snapped up.

Saul stood in the doorway of her bathroom. He inhaled deeply. "Followed that sweet smell all over town..." He took a step closer. His gaze drifted over her. "And straight back home to you."

Oh, hell. She'd been so worried about tracking Duncan that she hadn't even thought about Saul coming after *her*.

He snapped his teeth together. "That smell tempted me for weeks. Fuckin' *weeks*. Didn't even realize you were the one sending out that sweet scent, not until you came into containment. And now I've just got to take a bite."

The collar was around his neck. But the remote, hell, the backup remote she'd swiped on her way out of the lab was in her bedroom. In the nightstand drawer. Completely and totally useless to her at that moment.

Her hands were clutching the towel over her body. But it was weak protection. What she needed was a serious weapon.

Saul licked his lips. "Maybe I'll fuck you *and* rip your throat out, all at the same time..."

Oh, yes, Pate had made a real brilliant move in letting this psycho out of his cage. Brilliant.

She swallowed—four times—and managed to choke down her fear enough to say, "That alarm— it will feed back to the agency. P-Pate wired it. Agents will be here—"

He laughed. "I'm not as dumb as you think." He was totally blocking the doorway. And his claws were out. "I cut the wires leading away from this place. The alarm might be screaming in here..."

It was. Just like she was screaming in her mind.

"But no signal is getting out." He smiled at her, flashing his fangs. "No one's coming to save you. It's just you and me, sweets. You..." He jumped toward her and yanked the towel away. His claws sliced down her arm. "And me."

She didn't cry out at the pain. He wanted her to scream and beg. She could see it in his eyes. "You don't want to...do this."

He brought his mouth close to her neck. "I want nothing more. Your scent was in the air, did you know that? In the fuckin' ventilation. I smelled you all those days." His teeth raked over her skin.

She shuddered. *Stay strong. Focus.*

"Why do you smell so good?"

He hadn't changed into a wolf. That meant she had the advantage. His mistake. "You want to know why?" Her fingers lifted and pressed lightly against his shoulders. "Because I'm not human." Because she had a brew of drugs in her body that had tried to make her some weird mix of human and *vampire*. The drugs had the side effect of sending out that sweet smell. Vampires always smelled good, that was just one of the ways that they lured in their prey. But her scent had been amplified by the drugs. A bad side effect that she'd try to fix.

"What are you?" Saul demanded.

Instead of answering, she shoved him back, as hard as she could. He flew through the air, rammed through the doorway, and sent chunks of wood shooting up around him. She ran out after him. She wasn't sure how her strength would stack up against his, but she'd get the collar's remote and totally disable him—

He was already back on his feet. And between her and the nightstand.

Then he started to laugh. "Aren't you...full of surprises?"

Her breath was panting out. Her heart racing too fast.

And she was naked. Dammit, *naked,* in front of that psycho.

Her gaze darted to the nightstand.

"Ah...looking for this, are you?" He lifted the remote from his pocket.

*No.*

"Why don't you come and get it?"

Fine. She would. Time to see who was stronger...the beast or, well, *me.*

Holly pushed back her shoulders. Lifted her chin. Then bared her own fangs.

Saul's eyes widened.

"You should have stayed away," she told him.

He smiled at her. And crushed the remote in his hand.

Oh, hell. Holly swallowed, choking back her fear, then she attacked.

Holly raced across the room. This wasn't about testing herself. This was survival. Kill or be killed.

His claws sliced across her stomach. More blood flowed from her.

*No more.*

She grabbed his hands. Held them tight. Then her mouth went for *his* throat.

*Bite. Bite. Bite.*

The temptation that was always in her mind. Only this time, she wasn't resisting temptation.

"You fuckin' bitch, I'll slice you open, screw you while you bleed—"

It was his turn to bleed. Her teeth sank into his throat. His blood trickled over her tongue.

He howled. A loud, inhuman sound. He tried to shove her off him. They wound up both falling to the floor. She held on tight, not about to let him go. She *couldn't* let him go.

His blood was in her mouth. Werewolf blood. Powerful. Heady. The rumors she'd heard were true. She could already feel his blood making her even stronger.

He rolled, twisted, and came down on top of her. She kicked out at him, even as she kept her teeth in his throat.

He yanked his hands free from her grip. "Should have known...should have *known*..." His hands closed around her head, and he shoved her skull back against the floor. "*I know what you are.*"

Good for him. She knew what he was, too.

He lifted one hand. His claws glinted. "I know what you are...so that means I know how to kill you."

Hell.

And, right then, her alarm stopped its wild shriek.

He smiled. "Ready to die?"

*Again?* "No." Her chin lifted. "Are you?"

# CHAPTER FIVE

He followed Saul's scent—sweat, animal, fear—back to a small building on the outskirts of the city. From the outside, the place looked like an old fire station. One that someone had converted into a house?

He inhaled deeply. Saul had sent him on a wild hunt. Racing in and out of buildings, in alleys, through a tangled maze that had led through the city...

And back here.

His nostrils flared as he pulled in the scents around him. The musky scent of Saul and—

*Honey.*

Fuck, no. He ran for the building, his heart pounding frantically in his chest and his claws bursting from his fingertips. He lifted his foot to kick in the door, but saw that someone had already beaten him to that chore—the door's lock was broken. Shattered. He shoved the door open and rushed inside. The bottom floor was empty, but he could hear sounds coming from upstairs. He flew up those stairs, four at a time. Turned to the left—

And saw Saul, on the floor, on top of a naked Holly. She was bleeding. Saul's claws were out. He was trying to swipe at her.

Duncan roared.

Saul's head whipped up. His eyes locked on Duncan, then those eyes widened in horror. Before Saul could leap to his feet, Duncan had him. His hands locked around Saul's shoulders, and he yanked the shifter away from Holly. Then he slung the bastard against the nearest wall. The whole building seemed to shudder at that impact.

"Duncan!" Holly's voice was shocked, scared, and angry as she called his name. He turned back toward her. Pale flesh. Wide eyes. She was trying to cover her breasts with one arm and cover the juncture of her thighs with the other even as she *bled* from the gashes in her side and on her arm.

He reached for her.

And felt claws drive into his back.

"No!" Horror was the only thing he saw in Holly's eyes then.

The hands that had been reaching for her balled into fists. "Run." He could barely manage to get the word out.

She shook her head, sending her wet hair flying over her shoulders.

"Run!"

He spun back around and grabbed Saul's hand. With one twist, he broke the bastard's wrist. *Payback, you SOB.* Then he grabbed Saul's other hand and broke that wrist, too.

Saul staggered back. Then he hit the floor. Fur burst along his skin as his bones snapped.

Saul was shifting, and...*so am I.*

The white-hot agony ripped through Duncan. Speech was impossible. He could only snarl and growl as his body reshaped. His muscles tore, his tendons stretched. When his hands hit the floor, they almost instantly became paws. Power beat through him. Power...and bloodlust.

*He attacked what is mine.*

Mine.

Duncan went for the other wolf's throat. His paws slammed into Saul's side, and his teeth snapped at the bastard's neck.

But Saul's claws drove into Duncan's side. Sliced deep. The pain just made him angrier. Duncan attacked with his own claws. Blood matted Saul's pale coat of fur.

"Duncan?" Holly's quiet voice.

*Mine.*

He sank his teeth into Saul's neck.

"Duncan, we need him alive!"

No, they needed him to die. Because he'd hurt Holly. Not once—

Holly's arms wrapped round Duncan. "Please."

His whole body vibrated, but he hesitated, barely managing to hold back from taking the other wolf's life.

That hesitation was all that Saul needed. He staggered away from Duncan and ran for the big, bedroom window. The glass shattered as he jumped right through it, leaping out and falling to the street below.

Duncan jerked away from Holly and ran to the window. He stared below, snarling, as he watched the white wolf streak away.

"I don't have any close neighbors," Holly said quietly from behind him, "so I don't have to explain to anyone why a wolf just jumped out of my second story window."

He glanced back at her. The rage still burned within him, and he wanted to follow Saul but—

*Can't leave her.*

It wasn't just the wolf's instinct to protect. It was the man's, too.

Only she wouldn't be seeing him as a man. Just as a beast. He turned toward the window once more.

"Don't leave me," she whispered.

His muscles trembled. Didn't she understand? If he stayed—

"Please."

She broke him.

He whirled toward her. Fought to pull the man back to the forefront and shed the body of the beast. He wondered if the pain of the shift would become easier to bear, or if it would always feel like he was being ripped apart.

But the pain, it didn't last. In moments, he was one the floor, body trembling, hands and knees pressing against the hard wood of her bedroom.

"Duncan?"

His head lifted as the floor creaked beneath her footsteps. She'd grabbed a robe and wrapped it around her body. Her blood had stained the side of the robe.

He still wanted to rip Saul apart.

"It's okay." She kept talking softly and held out her hand, as if to a wild beast.

*Oh, yeah, right. That'd be me.*

"Are you...in control?" Holly asked, voice hesitant.

He was still on the floor. He should be on his feet, helping her. She was wounded. She needed care and attention.

But he didn't move because he wasn't sure of himself. He gave her the truth, simply saying, "No." Rumbling. Deep.

Her eyes widened.

He'd told her to run before. Why hadn't she listened to him? Saul hadn't been the only threat to her.

"I'm okay," she told him. Still in that whole let's-tame-the-beast voice. Only she didn't seem to get that the beast wasn't in the mood to be tamed.

Then she lifted her robe, revealing the curve of her thigh, the dip of her stomach. "See...all healed."

There were no wounds on her, nothing to blemish that smooth skin. How the hell was that even possible?

But...screw the how's...her legs were long and perfect. He could see the curve of her breast. She was trying to pull the robe back but—

*Want to see.*

In an instant, he was on his feet. His hands were on her, reaching for that robe.

"Duncan?"

"I told you...run..." She could still get away. He was as much of a monster as Saul and—

Holly shook her head. Her eyes seemed to see into him. "I don't want to run from you."

His breath was coming too hard. His heart racing too fast. His cock aching too much. He stood before her, naked because his clothes had shredded with the shift, and there was no hiding his arousal.

She wasn't pulling away. Wasn't pushing against him.

She was reaching up. Standing on her tiptoes. Kissing him.

The woman had just sealed her fate.

*You should have run. Now there won't be any escape.*

She tried to make the kiss soft and gentle. Not happening. He was on fire for her. Needed her more than air. So his hold was too rough, his hands almost shaking as he lifted her up against him and plundered her mouth. His tongue thrust past her lips. He tasted.

*Yes.* She tasted as sweet as she smelled. His mouth pressed harder against hers, and he stumbled forward with her.

They fell onto the bed.

His hands pushed between them. He didn't take his mouth from hers. Couldn't. He kept kissing her. And he ripped her robe. It tore beneath his claws.

*Claws.*

He still had claws. Hell, *no,* he couldn't hurt her. He yanked his mouth from hers. Tried to pull away from her.

"You can't leave me now," she said and pulled him back.

Duncan shook his head. His control was razor thin, and she didn't understand how dangerous he was. "I'll...hurt..."

It was all he could manage. He kissed her again. Drove his tongue past her lips.

*No. Pull away. Get away.*

Her hands curled around his shoulders. She arched against him. Her breasts were tight peaks. They rubbed over his chest, and his cock jerked in eagerness.

But he couldn't touch her. He had claws. He'd slice open her skin. *Can't.*

Her hands were sliding over his back. Soft, a silken touch. Helplessly, Duncan stretched into her touch.

Her legs were parted, with his much more powerful thighs between hers. They'd fallen this way when they tumbled onto the bed.

She was...aroused. He could smell the rich, heady scent.

He kissed a path down her neck. Licked her skin. His hands were flat on the bed, on either side of her. He wouldn't touch her with his hands.

Only his mouth.

She shivered beneath him. "You won't hurt me."

How was she so confident? He wasn't. He just knew that it was too late to pull back now. The beast wouldn't let him.

The man wasn't strong enough to leave her.

His mouth lingered on the curve of her shoulder. He had the strongest urge to bite her there. To...mark her.

His teeth nipped her.

She moaned.

The thunder of his heartbeat drummed ever faster in his ear.

The nightmare that had become his life, the agency, Saul—none of that mattered.

Only Holly.

Her nipples were a light pink. He put his mouth on one tight peak. Kissed. Sucked. Licked.

"Duncan!"

He loved the way she said his name. His fingers fisted on the bed covers. She was positioned so perfectly beneath him. All it would take was one deep thrust. He could already feel the wet heat of her arousal on the head of his cock.

One hard thrust.

He licked her nipple once more and then started to kiss his way down the curve of her stomach.

But her hands locked around his shoulders. "I need—"

His head snapped up. His eyes locked on hers. Whatever she needed, he'd give her.

"I need you," she whispered, wetting her lips. "I can't wait...please, Duncan!"

The roaring in his ears told him that he couldn't wait either.

The covers were tearing beneath his claws.

Her legs lifted. Curled around his hips, and her body arched toward him.

He drove into her, as deep as he could go. She gasped. He fucking growled. Then there was no holding back. There was only taking. Only pleasure. She was so tight around his cock. Squeezing. Hot. Perfect. He pulled back, thrust hard, again, over and over. The pleasure built, his spine tightened, his cock swelled even more.

He bent to kiss her. Tasting her even as he took her. And it was incredible. She was incredible.

Her sex squeezed even tighter around him. Holly pulled her head away from him, her breath heaving. Then she was kissing his neck. He felt the light rasp of her tongue on her skin.

She shuddered beneath him. Her body seemed to stiffen, and he knew her climax was close. So was his. He knew—

Her teeth sank into his neck. The bite shot a bolt of pure pleasure rocketing through him. He came, exploding within her on a release that was more powerful than anything he'd ever experienced.

His hips pistoned against her. He drove hard, plunging deep within her, as the pleasure hollowed him out.

And she was with him. He felt the ripples of her release. The contractions of her sex, and those small movements just increased his pleasure.

He could barely breathe, and he didn't care.

The sex was that good.

Then she was licking his neck. Her fingers were falling away from his shoulders. The thunder of his heartbeat finally slowed down, and Duncan forced his head to lift.

Her cheeks were flushed. Her eyes wide, but not sated—*scared.*

Duncan frowned. *What the hell?*

"I'm so sorry," Holly whispered and a tear leaked down her cheek.

He bent and licked that tear away. "Can't be sorry..." His words rasped out, "for sex that good."

Her lips parted. His gaze dropped to her mouth, and he saw that her lips were red.

Wet.

Not from his kiss because that redness...

Her tongue swiped out, and she licked a drop of moisture away.

That redness was blood.

Unease snaked through him. "Holly?"

He could see the edge of her canines, peeking out beneath her top lip. Her canines were longer, sharper than before.

*She'd bit my neck.* The pleasure had exploded then, and he hadn't cared about anything else.

"I'm sorry," she whispered again as she shoved him back.

Holly was far stronger than she should have been.

With the distance between them, he immediately missed the warmth of her body. Wanted back *in* her body. The pleasure they'd shared had just been the start. He wanted more. Much more.

*She had fangs.*

He stood on the side of the bed. The covers he'd ripped were in his hands, dangling from his fingers.

*She healed too quickly.* The slashes on Holly's side and her arm were gone, and now that he wasn't thinking so much with his cock, he realized that her wrist wasn't broken. Not even bruised.

She grabbed for some of the covers—the ones he hadn't ripped—and wrapped them around her body. Her eyes looked even darker than before.

*She'd had blood on her lips. Blood she'd licked away.*

He probably shouldn't have found that move sexy. He had. He found everything about her sexy, even the fact that—

"You're a vampire," he said.

She flinched, but, after a brief moment, Holly nodded.

His heartbeat—which had just slowed— slammed right into his chest. *What. The. Fuck.*

"I guess you're not the only monster in the room," she whispered.

He was on her in less than a second's time. He leapt back to the bed. Caged her with his body. "You're not a monster."

She was beautiful. Sexy.

And a vampire? Since when?

Did Pate know? Hell, he *had* to know.

"Yes." Her smile was sad. "I am." Her little fangs were still peeking out. Her gaze dropped to his throat.

His fingers rose. Touched the skin. It felt slightly tender, but that little pain was a small price to pay for the avalanche of pleasure she'd given him. As soon as she'd bit him, he'd come. And kept coming...until her mouth left him.

"I-I need to get dressed."

Duncan shook his head. The haze of lust and rage had cleared enough for him to think. Mostly. "You're not going anywhere." He finally had Holly just where he wanted her. Naked. In bed.

Her lashes lifted. Her gaze locked on his. Narrowed. "You don't want to push me now."

Actually, that was exactly what he wanted to do.

Except he heard the squeal of brakes outside. The cavalry? Finally coming to the rescue?

Car doors slammed.

Footsteps thudded as people raced toward her house—and *into* her house.

"*Holly!*" Pate's voice. Desperate. Afraid.

Horror widened Holly's eyes. "No, he'll find us...like this..."

So?

Her gaze flew around the room.

The agents—and it was more than one, probably three, judging by those thudding footsteps—were rushing up the stairs. There wasn't time to dress. Wasn't time to do anything but jump out of the bed and spin toward that door. Only he'd pretty much splintered the wooden door to hell and back when he'd burst inside before.

"Stay out!" Duncan yelled.

But Pate was already there. Staring at him with wide eyes, then looking over Duncan's shoulder. "*Holly?*"

The shock in his voice had Duncan's shoulders tensing. He put his body in front of Holly. "I said...*stay out*." The wolf's growl rumbled in those words.

But Pate must have been having one real slow night. Because he just stood in the doorway. Shane was behind him, craning his fool neck to see inside.

"Holly, what have you done?" Pate asked her, voice wooden.

Duncan didn't move. Holly did. He heard the faint rustle of her movement and then her hand was on his shoulder. Her fingers trembled.

Pate pushed into the room, shoving the broken door out of his way.

Holly's nails dug into Duncan's skin.

"Take another step," Duncan said, "and you'll regret it."

Pate stiffened. He held up his hand, indicating that Shane should move back. "Go downstairs. Wait with the others."

Shane hurriedly stepped back and got out of there. Good. Shane wasn't a complete dipshit.

"You're the one who's going to regret this," Pate said. He had a gun out. One that was aimed at Duncan's chest. Were those bullets made out of silver? Or wood? Those were the two prime choices for agents in their unit. "You should have never touched her."

"Pate!" Fear tinged Holly's voice.

"Did you drink from him?" His voice was hushed.

So Pate *did* know.

But that whisper said he didn't want Shane and the other agent to find out Holly's secret.

"She did," Duncan answered, cocking his head. *And I loved it.* Who would have thought? The bite of a vampire...

It could be one major turn-on.

"Why aren't you shocked?" Pate demanded. That gun was still pointing right at Duncan.

"From the look of things, you just screwed a vampire."

And it was the way he said it that pissed off Duncan. The anger, that tightly leashed fury.

"Watch it," Duncan warned him. His beast had been calmed by Holly's touch, but the wolf was ready to come out again.

"You just turned into an alpha! *Sonofabitch*! Don't you know what this means? You had sex with her—" Pate's eyes widened as he broke off. "She bit you." Muttered. He took another step toward them. "Did you bite her, too?" Intensity sharpened his words.

That gun was too close to comfort, and he was real tired of being on the receiving end of Pate's rage.

Duncan lunged toward him and snatched the gun right out of Pate's hand. He was getting rather used to his werewolf speed. "Don't point that damn thing at me or her again."

Holly laughed behind him. The sound was cold. Bitter. Not at all like her.

*But how much do you know her? You didn't even know she was a vampire.* The insidious whisper slid through his mind.

"Pointing the gun at me isn't the problem." She'd wrapped the sheet around her body, sarong style. Her hair had dried. Her cheeks were still flushed, and her skin seemed to shine. She was, without a doubt, the most beautiful thing he'd ever seen. "A few hours ago, he shot me in the heart with one of his wooden bullets."

And Duncan remembered the thunder he'd heard as he'd given chase after Saul. He'd been rushing through the woods, so intent on his prey that he hadn't even paused at that sound. He hadn't thought—Holly—

A snarl broke from his lips.

Pate's eyes widened. "Easy. It only killed her for a few minutes."

*A few minutes...*

"You're not freaking out because you just screwed a vampire." Pate still seemed confused by that point.

His back teeth locked. "I'm a werewolf. Who the fuck am I to judge?"

But Pate's eyes had gone back to Holly. "There's no going back now." His voice was almost sad.

Her chin lifted. "You never understood. There was *never* going to be any going back. No matter what you hoped." Then she headed into what looked like a bathroom. The doorframe was broken, and he could see some tile inside.

Pate's gaze followed her.

"Eyes over here, asshole," Duncan growled.

Pate's green stare cut to him. "Could you get some damn clothes on? Or my *eyes* will be going blind."

"I shifted," Duncan gritted. "She was in trouble—"

"Oh, yeah, I see that."

"There wasn't time to take my clothes off. I had to rush to her."

"I'm sure you did."

"And it's not like there are backup men's clothes here."

Pate's lips twisted. "Sure there are." He spun on his heel and headed out the broken door. His hand waved toward the right as he pointed down the hallway. "Second door on the right. Check the top drawer of the chest."

What?

"When you're both dressed, drag your asses downstairs," Pate said, the words an order from unit's director.

Duncan stalked down the hallway. Went in the second door on the right. He yanked open the drawer and pulled out a pair of jeans. They fit perfectly, as did the faded t-shirt. They had to belong to a guy near his size. *Who the hell was he?* And they—

They smelled like Pate.

*There's no going back now.*

Duncan slammed the chest closed. The wood shattered. Pate's reaction had been too personal. He'd known Holly's secrets. His clothes were in her spare bedroom.

*Mine.* The wolf started to claw inside of him.

Carefully, slowly, Duncan sucked in a deep breath. He could still taste Holly, only now...now her scent was blending with Pate's.

He stalked from the room and saw Holly. She had already dressed. She had on jeans that hugged her ass too well and a loose top. Her hand was on the banister, and she was near the foot of the stairs.

Pate was reaching for her. Curving his hand around her shoulder.

There was no sign of the other agents. Just Pate. Just Holly. Pate pulled her close against him. Held her.

Duncan's eyes narrowed. Pate was whispering to her, and when he focused hard enough, Duncan could just make out the guy's words.

*I'm sorry. We'll make it work. Everything will be fine again, I promise.*

Holly shook her head. Tried to pull away from him.

But Pate just tightened his hold around her. His lips brushed over her forehead. *I won't lose you.*

Oh, hell, yes, he would. Duncan bounded down the stairs. "Get your hands off her." A lethal order.

This wasn't about getting an order from his unit's director. Wasn't about the supernatural nightmare that was his life.

This was about some prick having his hands all over the woman that Duncan wanted.

And Pate needed to back the hell up before Duncan wrecked his face.

"I was worried this would happen," Pate said with a sigh. He didn't let Holly go. Big mistake. "Don't you see, Holly, he's linking with you? Bonding?"

"My fist is going to bond with your face," Duncan promised.

Holly pushed Pate away. Then she whirled to face Duncan. She blocked his path, stopping him before he could carry through on that sweet promise he'd made to Pate.

"Don't," she said, shaking her head.

He reached out his hand. Ran his fingers over the spot that Pate had kissed on her forehead. He needed to get some things clear, fast. Wolves... *werewolves* didn't react like humans.

Pate had that bit right. Duncan *was* linking with her. He wanted her again. Wanted her naked and screaming beneath him. She hadn't screamed with pleasure before, would she next time?

"My bite...it's...ah, making you react this way," Holly explained, her words rushed.

The bite?

"It...creates a connection. Between vampire and prey. There's pleasure in the bite."

Yeah, he'd gotten that part.

"The pleasure is addictive. It's how vampires lure their prey to them, again and again." Her lips tightened. "The vampires who aren't interested in torturing their prey, that is."

So the bite itself was the vampire's weapon?

"You shouldn't have bitten him," Pate snapped from behind her. "You shouldn't have—"

"I bit Saul first, okay?" Her shoulders had straightened. Her eyes were still on Duncan, but her words seemed to be for Pate. "Because your little wolf—the one you were so confident you could control—came to attack me."

Over her shoulder, he saw Pate's face. His expression had frozen into a stone mask.

"I bit him, then Duncan came in and chased Saul right out of the window." Her breath eased out. "Thank you, Duncan."

His hand fell away from her. "You should have let me kill him."

"That would have been a mistake." From Pate. Why was he still talking?

"Yes," Holly agreed with a nod. "It would have." Then she looked back at Pate. "The chip in the collar will let us track him. As soon as we do, I-I can get Saul to take us to the other alpha."

"Are you in control?" Pate gritted.

"Hell, yes," Duncan snapped. "Right now, I'm—"

"Not you, McGuire."

Holly's laugh broke what was left of Duncan's heart. "Does it matter? I took the blood, from both of them."

Pate frowned at her.

Duncan knew about vampires. Vampire 101 had been an introductory class for every agent entering the unit. He knew that the basic rules when dealing with a vampire went this way...

Rule number one: Don't get bit.

*Too late.*

Rule number two: If you do get bit, get the hell away from the vamp. Because once a vamp bit his prey—her prey—that vampire could slide into the victim's mind. Could command. Control.

*I am so screwed.*

Rule number three: Don't fucking get bit.

How had Holly become a vampire? Because from everything he'd heard, the transformation wasn't easy. A human had to be at the brink of death, and then the human had to get a very powerful infusion of vampire blood to make the transition.

"Isn't this why you made me?" Holly asked quietly.

Wait, hold up, *made* her?

"Get me to Saul, and I can deliver the alpha to you."

Duncan's gaze drifted between them as anger pulsed inside of him. "If all you had to do was take a bite of Saul, why not just do it back at the lab?" His hands fisted. He'd been running for *hours* as he tracked Saul. "Why send me on this whole song and dance about—"

"Biting him wasn't an option. Not if Holly ever hoped to return to her human life." Pate ran a shaking hand over his face. "Until you, she'd never taken blood from a live source. Only gotten transfusions of blood that had been injected with karahydrelene."

When Holly had followed him into the woods, he'd gotten too close to her. He remembered Holly's lips being crushed against his own. Remembered the faint coppery taste that had filled his mouth. His blood?

"I-I must have bit your lip when we kissed." Holly's gaze wouldn't meet his. "I'm sorry."

He wasn't. Maybe he should have been.

"Then, after Saul, when we were—" Her breath sighed out. "Werewolf blood has a very powerful effect on vampires."

"It makes them drunk with pleasure and power," Pate added as his hands crossed over his chest.

"I couldn't stop myself," she said, and finally, her gaze came back to his. "You were too good."

Uh, yeah, he'd thought the same thing about her.

"The karahydrelene worked to combat the changes occurring within Holly—" Pate began.

"Kara—what?" Duncan wanted to know. He'd never heard of it.

Holly gave him a small smile. "Karahydrelene. It's a drug I made that inhibited the bloodlust. With it, I could go for much longer periods of time without needing blood. My fangs never extended, and all of my other vampire...features...were contained."

"But now that she's just had straight werewolf blood..." Pate let his words trail away.

Holly's gaze held Duncan's. "The bloodlust is going to be much harder to control." Her gaze dropped to his throat. "Before you go out on this hunt with me, you need to know that. I might—I might try to drink from you again."

*Will you try to fuck me again, too?* Because he thought that would be a rather awesome bonus.

"Can you handle that?"

She stared at him with fear in her dark eyes. As if she actually expected him to say that a little bite from her was too much for him to handle. Um, hell, no, it wasn't too much. "Just so you're warned, too." He bent his head over hers. Caught more of her heady scent and didn't even care if the scent was part of a vampire's appeal to draw in her victims or if it came from the karahydrelene or if it was just *her*. "I may want my own bite."

"*No!*" Pate's immediate snap. "That can't happen!"

He didn't want to leave Holly but, slowly, Duncan made his way over to his boss. "You got a claim on her?"

"Uh, Duncan..." Holly began, voice rather nervous, from behind him.

Pate glared at him. "Yes, I do."

He could rip the man apart. The werewolf strength that he'd hated before was an advantage right then. "Forget it. You're not having her, you can just—"

"She's my step-sister."

Duncan managed to keep his jaw off the floor.

"And she's too good for you. So don't even think about biting her because she's not going to be your mate. Not going to be anything to you. You do the mission, and it's over. You've already screwed things up enough for her." A muscle jerked in Pate's jaw. "So have I."

Then Pate marched away, leaving Duncan staring after him. He knew the guy was right, on one count anyway. Holly was too good for him. That was why he'd stayed away from her before the werewolf attack. And even though he knew that Pate was right in warning him off, Duncan also knew that he wasn't about to leave Holly. They'd complete the mission all right, but after that, things would be far from over between them.

# CHAPTER SIX

The bar was loud. Bursting with noise. Laughter. Music. The scent of alcohol and sex lingered in the air.

So did the scent of blood.

From the corner of her eye, Holly glanced over at Duncan. They'd followed the signal from Saul's collar, but, honestly, she thought Duncan could have tracked the guy without it. His senses were seriously amped, and she was pretty sure that those enhanced senses could tell that—

*I'm still turned on.*

Because she was. No wonder Pate had tried to keep her away from werewolf blood. It was heady. Saul...Saul's blood had amped up her body. Given her a boost that made her feel incredibly strong.

But Duncan's blood? It had been like wine. Ecstasy. Her whole body had shuddered from the pleasure of tasting it.

She looked at him now and still wanted.

It was wrong on so many levels. She was on a mission. Her first, ever. This was her chance to show Pate that she could still be an asset, even as a vampire. That he didn't have to keep hiding her in the lab with the karahydrelene-laced blood right by her side in case she had a meltdown.

This was her shot, but she was about to blow it because she kept lusting over the werewolf to her left.

"Can you control me?"

The quiet question was the last thing she'd expected. Her head turned fully toward him. They were across the street from the bar, waiting beneath a broken streetlight. The darkness surrounded them, and, though she knew he could see perfectly in that darkness, Holly could only see the outline of his body and face.

Vamps didn't get the sensory kick that werewolves possessed. They got the enhanced strength and mind control bit instead.

"Can you?" Duncan pressed.

"I haven't," she said, hedging.

A rough laugh. "That means you could, if you wanted."

Yes. Maybe. "I should confess something to you." She'd sounded so confident with Pate because she'd *had* to sound that way. "I, uh, I've never tried to control anyone before."

A rather painful silence, then, "Run that by me again." His eyes were shining, like a cat's, in the dark.

"I've only taken blood from you and Saul. The other blood—it came bagged or was given to me via an IV. There were no people there for me to try and control." Her words tumbled over each other. "Theoretically, I should be able to do this. I mean, it's something all vamps can do so—"

He swore, grabbed her arm, and pulled her into the nearest alley. Then he pushed her back against the rough brick wall. "*Theoretically*?

Holly, this isn't some experiment. You go up to that werewolf and you *can't* control him, then he's gonna go right for your heart."

Or her head. Because one surefire way to kill a vamp? Take off the head.

"I can do this, okay?" Her heart was racing in her chest. His hands had curled around her shoulders and his head—and that sexy mouth of his—waited just inches from hers.

"Prove it." His hold tightened on her. "You got my blood, and you got his. So if you can control me..."

"Then I can control Saul." But she shook her head. "I don't want to do that to you."

He stared down at her.

"You've been through enough lately. It's just been over thirty-six hours since your change. I know what it's like to have your life ripped away." Oh, talk about being able to relate. Now she could finally tell him. "And I'm so sorry this happened to you." Holly pulled in a deep breath. "That's why I'm not going to control to you. You don't need me ripping into your mind, too."

His hold tightened. He brought his head even closer to hers. "I want you in my mind."

"Duncan—"

"If you can't do it, then you aren't going into that bar. I'll call Pate. Tell him to come get you. Tell him the operation is off."

Then what would happen to her? She'd get shoved back in her lab, and Pate would start forcing her to try his cures again.

"Make me step away from you." Duncan's words were a low whisper. Rumbling. Dark. Sexy.

"You think that you linked with me when you took my blood? Then make me step back. That's simple enough, right?"

Yes. But she hated the thought of forcing him to do anything, even something so small, against his will.

"I'm inviting you in, baby. Let's see what you've got." His body brushed against hers. "Make me stop."

Then his mouth took hers. Light at first, then harder. His tongue skimmed over her lips. His hand slid down her body, his fingers skirting around the curve of her breast.

A moan rose in her throat.

Make him stop? She'd rather make him strip.

A door slammed. A car horn honked. Voices drifted toward them.

"Make me," he said against her lips.

She could feel his cock swelling against her. Her body ached but...

Holly pulled her mouth from his. "S-step away from me."

His whole body tightened.

Then his mouth found hers again as he kissed her harder.

Her heartbeat doubled. He wasn't supposed to still be kissing her. This wasn't the way it worked. She'd interviewed vamps at the facility. They'd all said...

*Controlling prey is easy. Take the blood. Then just tell them what you want. They can't resist. The blood is the link. The power.*

They'd laughed about how easy it was to control humans.

Only...oh, crap, she wasn't trying to control a human. She was dealing with a werewolf. Maybe she couldn't control him through a compulsion.

He still had on his silver collar. Pate had given her another remote and had made sure it was tuned to be able to control both Saul and Duncan.

But she didn't want to use the silver to control them.

His mouth lifted from hers. "Do you know..." Duncan growled against her lips, "that I want to bite you?"

Vampires weren't the only ones who liked to bite.

"So what's to stop me?" he murmured. His fingertips were suddenly at her throat. Trailing lightly over skin. No, not just his fingertips. She could feel the light scratch of his claws.

"There's no one here. Just us. No other agents. No Pate." The last was said with a touch of anger. "I can bite you. I can claim you. And you can't stop me."

What could have been a lick of fear shot through her. But, no, this was Duncan. He wouldn't do anything to her.

Would he?

"S-stop," she said.

"Make me," he ordered her again.

His body seemed harder. Stronger. He wasn't shifting—oh, he'd better *not* be shifting.

"Duncan?" Yes, okay, fear had the word trembling.

"When a werewolf bites his chosen mate," and his fingers were on the side of her neck, "it's a mark that tells all the other wolves to stay the hell away. A mark that says...*mine*."

She knew how the wolf rules went. She'd done the paranormal classes that the agents took, too.

"I look at you," his words were deeper, darker, "and think...*mine*."

"You're trying to s-scare me." Trying. Succeeding.

"No. I'm telling you what is." His head lowered to her neck. His teeth skimmed over her frantically racing pulse. "You won't get away from me."

She didn't think it was the man who spoke the words, but the beast he'd become. The wolf inside that thought in primitive terms of possession and claiming.

Holly lifted her hands and tried to shove him back. "Stop." He couldn't claim her. A werewolf claiming was forever. Or rather, until death. Because werewolves had been known to kill their mates instead of letting them escape.

"*Make me*," he snarled.

His hold was so much tighter. Harder. His hips were pressing against hers, and she could feel the light sting of his teeth on her neck.

The situation was out of control. He was out of control. They were supposed to be working together. Getting Saul.

"Duncan..."

His head lifted. His eyes stared down at hers. They were glowing—the gold and blue so bright. Far more beast than man. In that instant, she knew that he wasn't stopping. Not unless she made him.

Her wild heartbeat shook her chest. She stared into his eyes. Felt fear and adrenaline heat her blood. "Let me go." Her words didn't shake. They just came from her, whispered softly.

His jaw clenched.

"Step away from me." Her heart raced faster. Adrenaline had her fingers trembling as she pushed against his chest. "And get your hands *off* me."

His teeth snapped together. And he backed away.

"*Get control of your beast,*" she said, flattening her hands against the wall behind her. "Get that control *now.*"

His shoulders rolled. His claws turned back into regular nails, and the wildness faded from his eyes.

They stared at each other, breath heaving.

*I did it.* But, just to be sure, she blurted, "*Tell me you love me.*"

"I love you," he said instantly.

And her heart hurt. "Right." Softer. She nodded. "I think that ends our little experiment, doesn't it?"

He blinked. His eyes were still feverishly bright, shining in the night.

"I guess I just had to be scared enough." Her head tipped back against the bricks as she stared up at the dark sky. "That was the purpose of that little scene, wasn't it? You were trying to scare me into losing control so I'd be able to use the vamp power?" Maybe that had been the key. He'd made her shake with fear for a moment there, but, it had worked. When she'd only had fear left, there had been no holding back. She'd felt as if something unlocked within her.

Power.

She realized that he hadn't spoken.

Her gaze darted to him. "Duncan?"

He shook his head. "I wasn't trying to scare you."

Uh, oh. All of the moisture seemed to dry up in her mouth.

"I wanted to take you." He backed up another step. "Consider yourself warned."

Crap.

He turned away from her. "At least you know how to stop me now."

He'd really been ordering her to stop him. Ordering...or begging? The words had been so rough. Had the man been fighting the beast? Trying to hang on? She reached out for him.

But he stepped farther away.

"No touching," he growled. "When I touch you, I *want*."

The blood link that she'd created? Or something more? Vampires were addictive to their prey, but she didn't just want to be some addiction to him.

*I love you.*

She wanted to be something more.

"Let's do this." He headed toward the mouth of the alley.

"Wait!"

He stiffened but didn't glance back. She forced herself away from the bricks. "Let me take off your collar." Pate had wanted him to keep wearing it. Because Pate didn't trust Duncan's animal instincts.

"That's not a good idea," Duncan said.

"You're not going to attack any human, you're not—"

"I almost attacked you. And with the full moon coming..." She saw his hands clench. "It's a risk I can't take."

Because of his family. She knew what had happened to them. The slaughter by werewolves that had left a five-year-old boy covered in blood and orphaned in the world.

He'd learned monsters were real at such an early age. Too early.

She hadn't learned that lesson until she'd stepped into Pate's world.

"I keep the collar." It rode low on his neck. "And you keep the remote." His head turned and his gaze met hers once more. "And if I ever go for your throat or your heart and you can't pull me back with a vampire compulsion, you don't fucking hesitate to burn me."

She could only stare at him in shock.

"Promise me," he demanded.

She nodded, but she couldn't bring herself to speak. Because she didn't want to lie to him.

Then they were heading toward the bar. Toward the laughter and the noise on the wrong side of the city. A battle waited for them, and this time, she would fight.

And not be the same victim that she'd been a year ago.

Because just a few blocks away, well, Holly had died in a spot there. In a pool of blood. With

a vampire standing over her and with her brother
screaming her name.

***

The bar reeked of blood and death. Humans
were inside, dancing, seemingly oblivious to the
smell.

But Duncan wasn't human, not anymore. His
nostrils widened as he pulled in the heavy scent
that came primarily from the door on the far left.
The door marked Private.

The door was guarded by two men he pegged
instantly as werewolves.

"What's happening in that room?" Holly
whispered from beside him as her fingers curled
around his arm.

He tried not to stiffen at her touch. He was too
aware of her. Of every single thing that she did.
Vampires were addictive, that was the spiel,
right? Maybe that was why he had a constant
hard-on and all he could think about was
plunging into her again.

*Mission. Focus on the mission.* He didn't even
know what in the hell had happened in that alley.
One minute, he'd been trying to get her to use a
compulsion on him. *Going out on a mission
without even a test run—what had Pate been
thinking?* And then in the next instant, he'd just
wanted to mark her. To let any other wolf know
that Holly belonged to him.

Because other werewolves would want her.
Especially once they got a whiff of her scent.

The old stories humans told about vampires and werewolves being enemies...those stories were wrong. Vampires and werewolves were often drawn together. One's strength was another's weakness. Together they were damn near unstoppable. So, hell, yes, another werewolf would want her.

He wasn't going to let anyone have her.

A blonde woman, laughing, drunk, was led to the Private door. The werewolves moved out of her way. Staggering a bit, she headed into the "Private" area. Her escort—a redhead with piercings circling his left ear—left her quickly.

The door closed behind her. The werewolves resumed their guarding position.

Duncan's eyes narrowed. The redhead started scanning the room once more. Looking for new prey.

"We need to get in that room," Duncan said.

"I figured that would be your answer." She sighed, then said, "All that blood...the humans they take in, they don't come back out, do they?"

No.

She pulled her hand away from him. "I'll get in. If Saul is down there—"

"He is."

"Then I'll get him to come back out."

Before he could stop her, she was sauntering across the room. The jeans she wore clung to her ass, and his gaze sure wasn't the only one to notice just how good she looked.

The redhead's stare locked on her.

He smiled.

*Touch her, and I'll break every bone you have.*

The beast was getting stronger within Duncan. So much more dangerous. Was it because the full moon was drawing ever closer? Or because he was destined to be one of those psychotic wolves that lived for blood and death?

The redhead had walked up to Holly. Gotten far too close to her. Duncan headed toward them. Even over the drone of voices, he could hear the redhead say, "You're new here, aren't you?"

"I heard it was a good place to party," Holly replied.

The redhead steered her toward the bar. Motioned to the bartender. "And do you like to party?"

"I like to get wild."

When had her voice become so throaty? Where was the shy doctor he knew and lusted after?

This was the vamp. Sexy. And taking too many risks.

The redhead was seriously leaning too close to her as the guy tried to give her a drink. "There's a real wild party downstairs."

Duncan caught the flash of her smile. "I didn't even know this place had a lower level."

"Um, yes, it's for VIPs." The redhead trailed his fingers over her shoulder. "I think you count as someone *very* important tonight." He lifted the drink toward her mouth. "Here, have some..."

The dick was shoving the drink down her throat. And Holly was what—just taking it? The woman had to be smarter than that!

And he realized that she wasn't actually drinking the dark red liquid. Her head turned a bit as her gaze met his.

Then she pushed the glass away. "Take me to the party," she told the redhead.

Huh. For her first mission, the lady was doing damn well.

Vamp power? Or just sex appeal? Either way, it was working.

The redhead was leading her toward the door. She had her entrance pass. Now for his turn. Because he wasn't about to let her go in alone.

The werewolves moved back for her, but Duncan saw them inhale deeply and frown at her. Hell. Her scent could blow things for them—

But then she vanished down the stairs.

The redhead immediately eased back. Started searching again.

Duncan kept his eyes on that door. His whole focus centered on the two guards there. If Holly wasn't back upstairs in three minutes, he would be going inside after her.

Three minutes.

He started to count.

*** 

The wooden stairs creaked beneath her feet. Holly's fingers slid over the wobbly railing, feeling the rough wood press against her skin. More music was coming from below. Pumping, hard music. She could hear women moaning.

The scent of blood was getting thicker.

Some party, all right.

Darkness waited at the foot of the stairs.

She headed into that darkness.

And was immediately grabbed by strong arms.

"I knew you'd come for me." The voice was familiar. Growling.

Saul.

He yanked her with him, pulling her through the darkness. She saw the flickering flames of candles burning. And...in that faint light, she saw a woman's broken body on the ground. Her neck had been ripped open. Blood pooled around her.

"The bitch reminded me of you," Saul said. His breath was hot against her throat. "I had to *bite*."

Fear shot her, and it was that wild, desperate fear that she needed. She twisted and put her hands on his chest. Stared into his hate-filled, wild eyes, and said, "Drop your claws." The claws that he'd dug into her sides.

He blinked. His teeth snapped together.

"Drop your claws!"

His claws fell to his sides. His body tensed, as if he were straining, and she knew he was trying to fight her compulsion.

"Now don't move. Not so much as a single step, understand me?"

He didn't move. Didn't reply. Didn't blink.

She figured he'd understood her.

Her gaze flew around that area. There was another door to the right. The faint moans were coming from inside that room. "What's happening in there?"

He didn't speak.

*"Tell me!"*

"Food."

That one word sent a shiver through her. She remembered the blonde who'd been led down the stairs just moments before her. "Is your alpha in there?"

Laughter. "You're...out of your league...little girl."

She surged forward. Her fingers wrapped around his throat. "I'm not a little girl." She bared her fangs. "I'm the woman who can kill you in an instant." She was itching to use that silver collar on him. Her gaze narrowed as she studied his neck. It was red and bloody—it looked like he'd been trying to claw the collar off.

No dice. Those things had been built to withstand just about anything. Pate had always been so clever with his gadgets.

"I'm asking again...is the alpha in there?"

*"Yes."*

There was no time to go for Duncan. The blonde would be dead in moments. "Stay here," she told him, knowing he'd have no choice. "And don't even *think* of shouting out a warning to anyone."

The mission was to get Saul. To have him take the agents back to the alpha who was leading the wolves on such a rampage through the human population.

But Holly wasn't about to leave a woman to die. She couldn't.

*I've been there.*

So she crept toward that room. Her palms were sweating when she opened the doorknob.

The door slid open. A fluorescent bulb flickered overhead. A woman was on a table, her blonde hair trailing around the table's edge. A man bent over her. His teeth were at her throat.

But he stiffened even as the door creaked open. His head lifted. His eyes—bright, glowing gold—met Holly's.

"Well, hello, there." He inhaled deeply and shoved away from the table. "Aren't you something...sweet."

Oh, shit. Was that the pick-up line that all the werewolves were going to use? As soon as she was back in her lab, she'd have to find a way to combat that scent.

He stalked toward her. He was big, as tall as Duncan, but with shoulders not quite as wide. His teeth were sharp, and his claws were definitely out.

"Harold said he'd be sending me some treats, but I had no idea..." he inhaled again, seeming to draw her scent fully into his lungs, "that a vampire was on the menu."

"I'm not," she snapped. Then, because she wasn't an idiot who'd come into this battle unprepared, Holly yanked out the gun that she'd tucked into the back of her jeans. A gun that Pate had given to her before she'd left her home. The gun wouldn't be loaded with wooden bullets—Pate would never risk giving her a weapon that could be used against her. Instead, she knew it would be packing silver.

The werewolf was just a few feet away from her. No chance that's she'd miss this shot. "Freeze," she told him. Technically, she didn't have a badge because she was the doctor on the team, not an FBI agent, but the wolf didn't know that. "Don't take another step," Holly ordered, "because you're under arrest."

He laughed at her. *Laughed.* Figured. Then he lunged toward her.

Holly's finger squeezed the trigger as she fired.

# CHAPTER SEVEN

When he heard the blast of gunfire, Duncan jumped away from the bar. The patrons had frozen and that gave him the perfect chance to rush right through the crowd.

Unfortunately, the werewolves at the door hadn't frozen. They'd ripped open that door and were already vanishing down the stairs by the time Duncan made it across the bar. He followed the sound of their thudding footsteps.

Then he heard another shot.

*Holly.*

He jumped over ten steps and landed on the bottom floor in a low crouch. The werewolves that he'd followed spun to face him. Duncan bared his teeth. They weren't getting in his way. No one and nothing would stop him from reaching Holly. The werewolves ran at him, attacking in unison.

Since they were attacking that way, so would he. He swiped out with the claws of his right hand and the claws of his left—catching both of those bastards with his attack. Blood flowed. They howled, then they hit the floor.

He kept running, heart pounding, as he tracked the sound of that gunfire. The rooms were dim, lit only with candlelight, but he didn't care. He could see perfectly.

He could sure as hell see Saul, standing frozen in the middle of the next room, with eyes wide and fangs glinting.

Duncan lifted his claws, more than ready to rip and tear again—

"Don't!" Saul yelled. "I'm not a fuckin' threat!"

The guy had fangs and claws. Like he'd buy that Saul wasn't about to attack him.

"Your vamp bitch..." Saul rasped the words, but didn't so much as take a step forward. "She *froze* me."

Duncan didn't know if he was lying or not, so to make absolutely sure that Saul wasn't gonna be an issue, Duncan slammed his fist into the guy's jaw as hard as he could. Saul's eyes rolled back in his head, and he hit the floor.

Duncan could hear the pounding of footsteps overhead. Humans, fleeing, but also...steps coming toward the basement room. Backup? If so, the agents needed to run faster.

He raced toward the room down the hallway. There were no more shots, but that didn't matter. Now he could smell Holly's scent, and he knew exactly where she'd be. *Hold on, Holly, I'm coming. Hold on.*

He knocked the door down. Went in with his claws out and a snarl on his lips.

Duncan saw a man on the floor. A man with dark hair and heaving shoulders. The guy's own claws appeared to be buried in his chest. Blood soaked the front of the man's shirt.

"I got him," Holly whispered.

Duncan's gaze snapped over to her. She stood to the left, about five feet away from the crouching man. She still had her weapon pointed at the guy.

Duncan hurried to her side. "Are you all right?" She didn't seem to be injured but—

The man's laughter stopped him. Chilled him. Because the laughter was cold, haunting, and strangely...familiar.

Duncan glanced back at him. The man's dark head lifted, and his glowing, golden eyes met Duncan's.

The werewolf's smile widened. "Hello, brother."

Duncan stiffened. "I'm not your brother."

Smoke was rising from the werewolf's chest. Now he realized why the guy's claws were in his chest. Holly had been the one shooting, and she'd fired the silver right into the werewolf. Now the fellow was trying to dig the silver out, with his claws.

The werewolf's head cocked to the right. His gaze swept over Duncan.

Duncan's own eyes narrowed. That guy...why the hell did he seem so familiar to him? Had they crossed paths before? "You're the alpha." Holly's shoulder brushed against his arm. Duncan wanted to grab her and pull her close, but that move would reveal too much to the predator that watched them with glowing eyes. Eyes that were searching for a weakness.

"So, it seems..." The man flashed fangs. "And so are you, *brother*."

That brother shit was getting old.

The werewolf inhaled deeply. His golden stare flickered to Holly. "Guess you got the first taste of her. But I'm sure there's plenty to go around."

Duncan lunged forward. In a second's time, he had his claws at the guy's throat. Holly was screaming behind him, telling him to back away, that she had this—

No, *he* had this. Duncan had the fool who thought he'd take what belonged to him.

"It's the way of the beast," the werewolf whispered to him. "We don't like to share what we've marked as ours, do we?"

*Holly is mine.*

The werewolf gave what appeared to be a sad shake of his head. "It's going to be a problem for you." Hell. It almost sounded like the psycho werewolf pitied him.

Duncan tightened his hold, ending the guy's words. "You don't threaten her. You don't even look at her."

Golden eyes stared back at him.

*I've seen those eyes.* He knew the man's face. The heavy cheekbones. The sharp nose. The cleft in the guy's chin.

He stared at the werewolf and heard echoes of screams. Cries that didn't come from anywhere but in his own mind. A child's cries. Begging. Desperate.

Holly's hands closed around his shoulders, and she jerked him back.

The screams died away as the alpha smirked up at him. Duncan could hear other sounds then.

Like the heavy tread of footsteps rushing toward the room.

Then Pate was there. Climbing over the broken door. Shane and Elias were right on his heels. They were all armed, and Duncan knew silver would be loaded in their guns.

"When will they turn those weapons on you?" The alpha asked, raising his brows. "Think they'll wait until the full moon rises? Or will they put you out of your misery before then?"

A woman moaned. The blonde in the back. The woman stretched out on a table and currently bleeding.

Was that blood having any impact on Holly? She seemed to be in control.

"I couldn't let him kill her," came Holly's soft voice. "I had to do something to stop him."

Her "something" had been to shoot the alpha. Nice.

Pate inclined his head toward Shane. The agent hurried across the room and scooped the blonde into his arms. But the blonde began to fight him almost immediately, crying out for "Connor!"

The werewolf's smile vanished. "We're done, love. The humans can take you now."

And just like that, she stopped screaming.

What the hell?

Shane carried her out of the room. Pate and Elias closed in on the alpha called Connor. Pate pulled a second weapon from a holster under his jacket. With one glance, Duncan knew it was the weapon used for dosing paranormals. Not killing, but knocking them out.

"Alpha, you're under arrest."

Connor's bloody claws raked over the dirty floor. "Gonna to send me to Purgatory?" His fangs snapped together. "Gonna toss me in a cage like you're doing with the rest of my kind?"

Pate fired the weapon. A dart burst from the gun and lodged in Connor's throat. "Yes."

"Y-your...mistake..." Connor grabbed the dart and yanked it from his neck. Duncan knew the removal would do no good. The drug was in his system now. "Putting...together...makes us...more dangerous..."

Pate fired again. Guess the guy wasn't in the mood to take chances. The second shot hit Connor in his already bloody chest. "Once you're in Purgatory, you won't be getting out."

Connor's gaze—now growing bleary—found Duncan. "N-neither w-will...he..."

Then he crashed forward, slamming into the floor. Out fucking cold.

Daphne and Brent—two other Para Unit agents—hurried into the room. They stood near Elias.

"Make sure he's secure, Elias," Pate ordered without taking his gaze off Connor. "I want his transfer to be smooth and fast. Get him to our base and get him caged."

The base that had already been under attack by the wolves? The place hadn't exactly been secure then, and Duncan sure hoped that Pate had stepped things up. The werewolves might try to rescue their alpha. If they did, he didn't want to walk into another bloodbath.

"The guards have been doubled. We aren't gonna have any trouble," Pate said, as if the jerk had just read his mind. But he couldn't do that. Pate was just human.

At least, Duncan thought he was.

"You didn't believe we'd have trouble before," Duncan said. He was suddenly conscious of his collar. The heavy weight. The silver that was burning more than it should in that instance. Because his wolf was trying to come out?

The alpha hadn't challenged him, other than that asshole comment about Holly. Shouldn't the guy have come at him with claws ready to rip him apart? The whole scene just felt wrong to him. What the hell was going on?

Duncan's eyes swept back to Connor. The unconscious wolf wasn't giving him any answers.

"Good job, Holly," Pate said. Duncan looked back as Pate's hand lifted, and he pulled the gun from her fingers. "But I thought I told you to locate him. To confirm that he was here, *then* call for backup."

"There wasn't time for backup." She shook her head. Duncan realized she was still staring at the unconscious werewolf. A faint furrow was between her brows. "He was going to kill the blonde."

"He won't be killing anyone else," Pate stated, as if making her a promise.

It wasn't a promise that Duncan was sure Pate could keep.

And just why did Pate still have his gun out?

Pate shifted his position slightly, as if putting his body between Holly and Duncan. No, not *as if* he were doing it. The guy was damn well trying to separate them.

He was also lifting his gun and pointing it at Duncan. "Is the silver burning you more now?"

"Why are you pointing that at me?" Duncan demanded, not answering the question.

A muscle jerked in Pate's jaw. "Because your eyes are glowing, and there's smoke rising from your neck." His lips tightened. "I didn't need to ask. It's obvious the silver is hurting you more. That wolf of yours wants out."

Because another alpha was close? Or because he'd been so wild at the thought of Holly being hurt?

Maybe it was both. And maybe...maybe it didn't matter anymore. "Drop the gun." Or he'd rip it out of Pate's hands.

Pate shook his head. "Before you go back to base, I need to make sure you're in control. If I need to cage you—"

"You're not putting him in a cell!" Holly snapped.

But Pate's steady gaze said that he would.

Perhaps Pate would do anything, if it kept a werewolf out of his sister's bed.

"Do you have control?" Pate demanded. It was the same question he'd asked Holly back at her place. It was time for the guy to stop worrying about the control of others and focus on himself.

Duncan leapt forward. He snatched the gun out of Pate's hands. Threw it across the room. "No, and neither fucking do you—"

It felt like a fist slammed into his back. A fist that was burning hot, then icy cold.

*That was no fist.*

His hand flew over his shoulder and closed around the dart that was embedded in his upper back. He yanked it out even as he spun and saw Elias.

Still holding his weapon.

"You...?"

"I'm sorry," Elias looked miserable. He swallowed, sending his Adam's apple bobbing. "You wouldn't *want* to hurt anyone, but you would. We know how the werewolves are."

Out to kill. Destroy. Savage.

His knees started to buckle.

Another dart hit him, this one fired from Brent's gun. Brent, the tall, silent agent who'd been the unit's newest recruit.

"What the hell have you done?" Holly's frantic voice. Then she was there. Wrapping her arms around him. Trying to support him. "Duncan? *Duncan!*"

His eyes were drooping closed. "Don't...cell..."

"I won't, I swear, I won't let them put you in a cell again. Duncan, just *stay with me!*"

He couldn't. The drug was in his system. Pumping fast and hard through his blood. The drug's effect wouldn't last long. Just long enough for Pate to toss him into a containment cell.

Before, he'd gone into a cell willingly, because he'd been afraid of what his beast might do.

This time, Duncan wondered if Pate had plans to make a cell his permanent home.

Was that what Connor had been trying to tell him? That he'd wind up in Purgatory, too? Now that he'd done the job Pate wanted, the director might not want him around anymore.

Too late, he was already in hell. He wasn't about to head out on a one-way trip to another prison.

"Duncan?"

He wanted to talk to Holly.

But all he could do was sink into the darkness.

\*\*\*

"This is a mistake!"

Yeah, right, Pate had been singing that same song for the last hour. Holly didn't look at him. She was too busy with her patient. Her *unconscious* patient, thanks to her brother. Duncan was on the exam table in front of her. Strapped down and still wearing his silver collar.

"The mistake was shooting one of your own men." *Jerk.* What had Pate been thinking? And Elias—Elias was supposed to be Duncan's friend. There should have been a rule there...friends didn't shoot friends in the back with paranormal knockout drugs.

The fact that she'd been the one to create that little brew for Pate to use on his missions? That just made her feel even more miserable.

"You saw him," Pate muttered as he paced behind her. "His eyes were glowing. The silver was burning his neck. I was afraid his control was shattering."

Because the full moon was coming ever closer.

"He had his control." Her fingers stroked over his arm. He felt so warm. Hot.

"And I don't have your confidence in him."

"He's your agent. You *should* have confidence in him."

"After the full moon...if I see that he can stay in control then...we'll talk about confidence."

There was something in his voice. A note that made her nervous. She glanced back at him. She and Pate were in her lab, so this was as much privacy as they were likely to get in the facility. "What are you planning?"

He shook his head.

Her gut tightened. "Pate?"

"It's all about the moon," he said.

The full moon that would rise with the coming night.

"After that, we'll see what happens. Who's a friend. Who's a foe." He stalked toward her. His hand lifted. Cupped her chin. "Don't take any more of his blood." A low whisper. "There's still time for you. I know there is."

No, there wasn't. "I can't go back."

He didn't want to admit it, but they both knew the human she'd been had died in that alley a year ago.

On the night when a monster had come for Pate, but had killed her instead. They'd been walking, heading toward a restaurant after watching a movie. Everything had happened so quickly.

A man had appeared and yanked her away from Pate. The stranger had sliced open Pate's stomach, then gone toward him with fangs bared.

"Do you ever wish you'd let him kill me?" Pate asked, voice quiet and emotionless.

Holly inhaled sharply.

And realized that they had an audience.

"Do you think about that night?" He continued, seemingly oblivious to the fact that the softest of rustles sounded behind them.

*Duncan was waking.*

"I-I try not to think about it."

Pate had been on the ground. Telling her to run. *Get the hell away! Don't look back!* His shout still rang in her ears some nights.

But he'd always been there for her. So she hadn't been able to leave him. She'd had no weapon. Just her fists.

She'd jumped on his attacker's back. Pounded him. Clawed him. Gotten his attention away from Pate.

The attacker had turned and smiled at her.

She'd screamed. *Fangs!*

Then those fangs had been in her throat.

"You're a terrible liar, Holly." Pate sounded sad. "You should have let me die."

"No." Instinctive.

The fangs had sliced deep into her throat. Her scream had died. He'd hurt her, so badly. She'd been the one on the ground then. He'd been over her, surrounding her. Gulping, slurping, making her so sick and afraid.

Then Pate had driven a stake into his back.

"Do you...do you ever wish that I'd put that stake in you, too?" His question chilled her.

She flinched. "No."

Some of the tension left his shoulders.

She knew how the vampire transformation worked. A vampire's victim had to be near death. Had to be drained, then given the vampire's blood. It was a virus. An infection. Science had perfectly explained it to her.

That night, the vampire hadn't been able to give her his blood. Not willingly, anyway.

The vampire had still been alive after Pate's attack. Alive, but weak. Pate had sliced open the vampire's wrist and had forced the guy's blood in her mouth before Holly could even think of turning away.

*You'll live. You'll fucking live.*

Only then had he ended the vampire's life. After she'd gotten her transfusion. She didn't really remember the specific details. She'd just opened her eyes to find that the vampire was missing his head.

*I don't want to think about that night.* She hadn't been lying about that part.

"It's over." Her lips felt numb. "There's no sense looking back."

"Sometimes, we can't go forward until we go back." His hand fell away from her chin. "I was selfish that night. I couldn't let you go."

She grabbed his hand. "And I wasn't ready to leave you."

His gaze held hers. They'd been together for so many years. She'd been three when her mother married his father. He'd been ten. A hero in her eyes. When their parents had died in an auto accident eleven years later, Pate hadn't let her go into foster care. He'd taken care of her. Always.

He could be an asshole sometimes. Overprotective. Too controlling. But he was family.

The only family she had.

"There is a cure." His voice shook. "It's a virus. You said it yourself. An infection. If you can catch it, you can cure it."

He wanted to think so.

She just didn't believe that was the case. The virus changed the body. Mutated it. With that kind of change, all of her research was showing that there was *no* going back. There might never be a cure. Instead, the best she could hope was treatment—that was what karahydrelene had done—treated the symptoms so that she could function almost normally.

She stepped away from him. "Duncan isn't going into a cell. I won't let you cage him."

Pate's gaze dipped behind her. "He'll go if he can't stay controlled."

She turned her head back to look at Duncan just as he snapped right through the bindings that held him. In an instant, he leapt to his feet. Hmm...he shouldn't have been quite so agile after the dosing.

Pate's gaze said he realized the same thing.

*Dangerous.*

As dangerous as a vampire. *As dangerous as me.*

Holly put her hand on Duncan's arm, stilling him before could get any closer to Pate. "He's *not* putting you in a cage."

"I won't do it," Pate agreed, but one eyebrow rose and he added, "I think you'll put yourself there." Then he headed for the double doors. "In case you're curious..." Pate said, throwing the words over his shoulder, "the other alpha is in Containment Area Five."

Then he was gone. Holly was all alone with her werewolf.

*Not mine.* Why did she keep thinking of him that way? Duncan wasn't hers. Was he?

"I'm sorry," she whispered. "I had no idea they were going to drug you."

His hands curled around her shoulders. He pulled her body closer, forcing her to face him.

Did he seem...um, bigger? *He did.*

"Duncan, I—"

His mouth was on hers. Hot. Hard. And she just decided to forget talking right then. She kissed him back, almost desperately, as her fingers locked around his arms and her nails sank into his skin.

He had her flush against his body now. That wonderful heat of his seemed to singe her right through her clothes. She could feel the heavy thrust of his arousal. Okay, yes, he'd come out of that drugged state *very* aware.

Her heart raced in her chest. Her body trembled. Not with any kind of fear, but with pure eagerness.

His head lifted. His eyes were shining. Definitely not the stare of a mortal man. She didn't care.

"Why aren't you afraid?"

*Because I'm as much of a monster as you are.*

He shook his head before she could think of a response that didn't sound so brutally cold. He wasn't a monster. Or...hell, she didn't think of him that way.

Even if she saw herself as the nightmare in the room.

"You're the only one I trust here," he told her.

Her breath rushed out. "Duncan..."

"Something's going on. Holly, I *know* that alpha."

"Well, you've been hunting in the city. You probably—"

"I've seen him in my nightmares."

That froze her.

"Werewolves killed my family when I was just a kid."

She knew that. That attack had been what had placed him on the path that led to Seattle's Para Unit. He'd wanted to protect others. To stop the same fate from knocking on their doors and leaving a trail of blood behind.

"When I look at Connor, I hear the screams from the attack."

She barely controlled her flinch.

Sometimes, when she looked at Pate, she could hear her own screams. *From my attack.* She'd tried to hide that weakness from him. Pate carried enough guilt on his shoulders. But after what she'd said minutes before, she knew that he already realized she saw hell when she saw him.

"I. Know. Him."

His arms were still around her. Her nails still digging into his skin.

"Help me," he said.

Holly nodded, and she knew that she could refuse him nothing.

*\*\*\**

Connor was caged and collared. And he looked pissed off.

Duncan marched into the alpha's containment area. Elias was stationed near the cell door. When he saw Duncan, Elias immediately straightened to his full height. "Jeez, I'm so sorry, man—"

Duncan lifted a hand. "If you're really sorry, then you'll give me ten minutes with this guy. You'll walk out, get yourself a drink, and not mention to anyone that I'm here."

Elias stared back at him. His partner's eyes—*ex-partner*—were guilt-ridden. "I'm sorry I couldn't kill you."

Connor started laughing from his cell. That bastard laughed a lot.

Elias shook his head. "I know it was what you wanted."

Death? Duncan glanced over his shoulder. Holly was behind him. It had been her security card that had gotten him access to this area. Seeing as how his access had been revoked.

But she'd come with him, not hesitating even a moment when he had to sound straight-up crazy.

*Maybe I am crazy.* Maybe the madness of the wolf was setting in, but right then, "Death's the last thing I want." He figured Elias needed the warning. Things had changed. Fucking fast. "You come at me with silver, and you could be the one to die."

Elias backed away from him. "But...your family..."

"Family..." A dark mutter from Connor. "Can't erase their sins, can't claw them to pieces."

Duncan frowned at him. Connor had risen and come to stand less than a foot away from the silver bars of his cell. Connor was the only prisoner housed in Containment Area Five.

Connor was rumored to have killed dozens of paranormals and at least eight humans in the Seattle area. All within the last year.

Psychopath? A psychopathic werewolf was a living hell on earth.

"Though I have tried the clawing technique a few times," Connor added as he glanced down at his hands. "Pity werewolves heal so fast."

Elias edged away from the cell. "Holly? You coming with me?"

"She stays," Duncan said immediately. He didn't want Holly out of his sight. No, more than that. He needed her close.

Wanted her close.

Elias's gaze darted between them. He and Elias had worked well together just days before, but in that moment, their camaraderie seemed long gone. Maybe it was due to the fear that lingered in Elias's stare. The hint of terror that he couldn't quite hide.

He didn't see Duncan as a man anymore.

"Ten minutes," Elias finally said, giving a hard nod. "And I'll...I'll make sure that no one gets through the door until you're done."

Duncan inclined his head. "Thank you."

Elias's hands fisted. "It could have been me. It *should* have been me. You saved my ass, and now look what you've become."

The thing he hated.

Only he didn't hate the power he could feel coursing through his veins, and even the wolf that lurked within him didn't seem so foreign now. It was actually as if he'd finally found a part of himself that had been missing.

"I'm sorry," Elias told him and turned away. "So damn sorry."

"Don't be." The flat words broke from him and caused Elias's shoulders to stiffen. "We all dig our own graves in this world." He'd made the decision to jump in front of those wolves. Elias hadn't forced him to do anything. Neither had Pate. Every decision had been his.

Elias's footsteps were soft as he left the containment area.

Holly's breath expelled in a rush when the door shut behind him. "Pate will know we're here. He'll see us on the security cameras."

True enough. "He wants us here." Why else would Pate have told him where to find the alpha? Pate never said or did anything without a reason.

Holly nodded. "All right then. It's your show."

His freak show, yeah. He turned from her and paced toward those bars. Connor stared back at him. Eyes narrowed. The werewolf should have been looking at him with hate, with fury, hell, maybe even with fear—the way Elias had been doing.

But there was no emotion in those golden eyes.

Time to make some emotion come out. "How do I know you?" Duncan demanded.

Connor shrugged. "Maybe I've got one of those faces." He smiled, but the smile never reached his eyes.

"When I look at you," Duncan continued, standing just inches away from the cell, "I hear screams. A kid crying." Connor looked like he was close to Duncan's age. Maybe a bit younger.

"I can't help what you hear." But Connor's smile had slipped a bit. "Can't help you at all."

Holly's footsteps padded closer. "I could...I could make him tell you what you want to know, Duncan."

Connor's stare drifted to her. Sharpened. "The vampire. The sweet bite I'd hoped to enjoy." He inhaled. "Don't you smell nice, just like honey and—"

Duncan's hand flew through the cage bars. His claws hung inches from Connor's throat. "I already warned you about her."

Emotion finally flashed in those eyes. Rage. "You think you're gonna mate with a vampire? Think you'll get all of that power to control?" He shook his head. "Better rethink that. You'll just make the same fucking mistake he did. And you'll leave the same bloodbath behind."

Duncan's heartbeat drummed in his ears. "Who are you talking about?"

Connor's gaze searched his. "Maybe you need to get the vamp to bite you. Get her to *make* you remember."

Connor was just jerking him around. Duncan yanked his hand back through the bars and barely felt the singe of the silver on his fingers.

"You believe you were the good guy, don't you?" Connor mocked as he rocked forward onto the balls of his feet. "The human out there, fighting the werewolves. Putting us in cages and sending the worst of the lot to rot in your Purgatory."

"I was *saving* humans." He wouldn't regret what he'd done. He'd never taken down any paranormal without proof that the man or woman had been killing humans. Never. "I don't throw innocent paranormals into cages. Every single one I captured was a menace. Someone who had to be stopped."

Connor's gaze was on Holly once more. "Are you going to be able to stop him, do you think? When the moon rises and the alpha werewolf really comes out, I don't even know if someone like you can control him."

Another one singing the song about him going moon crazy. Sure, it was a fear that Duncan had, but he was tired of everyone throwing it in his face.

"I trust Duncan," Holly replied, voice clear. "*He* will keep his control."

Connor shook his head. "You're a fool. The werewolf in him will come for you because he wants your blood and your body. And he'll kill anyone who comes between the two of you." He tapped his chin. "That's the way for mates, and whether your special agent werewolf wants to admit it or not, he's marked you as a mate."

Duncan could feel the glance that Holly cast toward him. He didn't look at her then, couldn't. Connor was telling the truth, and there was no point denying it. *I want her.* "I have ten minutes, and you're wasting my time." And not answering his questions. Deliberately, Duncan was sure. "Why do I see you and hear a child begging for help? Screaming my name?"

A muscle jerked in Connor's jaw. "You don't know me."

"I know your face." He just didn't know how. "I've seen it before."

Connor shook his head. "Let me guess...in your nightmares?"

Yes.

"Not all humans can become werewolves," Connor murmured. "You have to possess the DNA that will let you transform."

"I don't want a science lesson!" Duncan snarled. *Wasting time, wasting—*

"Where do you think the DNA comes from? It's no random mutation."

"It's passed down," Holly said, her body sliding closer to Duncan's.

Connor nodded.

"Werewolves and humans...we're separate, but we can mate. But the half-breeds...they can't always change," Connor murmured.

"The genetics are there," Holly explained to Duncan. "They would still pass down...in children, grandchildren."

Connor's stare was back on him. "We're everywhere, you see. The teacher in your school. The cop walking his beat."

*Me.*

"They're us, and they don't know it." His teeth snapped together. "Not until they get the bite."

"The bite must activate the dormant DNA." Holly's arm brushed his. "That's why some humans can change and others can't. Those who can...they've got an ancestor who was a werewolf. I should have realized it before. It's not about mutations—it's..." Her head turned and her gaze found his. Softer, she finished, "It's just family."

Duncan's hands fisted. His claws were trying to break free. "Werewolves *killed* my family."

"Is that what you were told?" Connor asked, words rumbling.

"It's what I saw." He glared at the wolf, glared and heard—*Help me! Duncan! Duncan!* A child's voice.

His eyes squeezed closed.

"Hearing voices are you? Those screams again?" Connor taunted. "Careful, or even your vamp will start to think you're going crazy."

His eyelids flew open. "I. Know. You."

"And I know you," Connor fired right back. In that instant, the mask he wore dropped. Rage burned fire-hot in his eyes as his fangs extended. "I know your face. I know your scent. I've looked for you...for *years.* And I found you, hunting me. Hunting our kind!"

"There's no 'our kind' here! Werewolves killed—"

Holly wrapped her arms around Duncan and pulled him back from the cell. "Elias is coming back."

The thunder of his heartbeat had drowned out the sound of approaching footsteps.

Connor's cheeks were flushed. His claws out. His chest heaving.

Duncan's claws were out. His chest heaving.

"Alphas aren't made," Connor told him. "We're born. One generation to the next. Alphas only come from alphas."

The door was opening behind him.

Duncan didn't look back. He couldn't. He remembered what Connor had told him when he'd burst into that basement room, so desperate to reach Holly.

*"Hello, brother."*

His eyes swept over Connor's face. "Have you gotten his DNA?" Duncan asked Holly.

"Yes. A sample was taken when he first came into the facility."

They had the best lab in the nation there. With equipment most couldn't even dream of.

Connor smirked at him. "Figuring it out, are you?"

*"How?"*

"The ten minutes are up," Elias said before Connor could speak. "And I just saw Pate in the hall. He's coming this way."

Because Pate would have been listening. He would have realized exactly what or rather, who, Connor was to Duncan.

"It can't be possible."

"What? That you were always the monster you hated? Trust me," Connor growled, "it's possible. Welcome to my nightmare."

"I don't have a brother." Why dance around this anymore? "Holly will check your DNA against mine, and this BS you're spilling won't fly."

But Connor just stared back at him.

"It won't. I don't have a brother."

Connor lunged forward in an instant. His hands wrapped around the silver bars and smoke rose from his flesh. "Because you let that bastard take me! I begged you to save me. I was four! Fucking four! You were supposed to watch out for me. You were supposed to save me!"

Duncan couldn't speak.

"You let him take me." Connor's gaze slid to Holly. "Now I'll take everything from you."

Holly had stiffened beside him.

"The hell you will," Duncan snarled. No one was taking Holly. No one was hurting her.

"It's already started," Connor said, voice lowering. "You don't even realize it. The moment you were bitten...it was all planned. Your humans? They sold you out. They gave you to me. This time, you'll be the one to scream and beg. And there will be no one to save you—or her."

# CHAPTER EIGHT

They were brothers. Duncan and Connor. She'd done testing, and the proof was right there for her to see. They shared the same father.

*Alphas are born, not made.*

Their father had been a werewolf alpha, and now, so were both Duncan and Connor.

The two men also shared the same mother. She'd been lucky enough to get DNA from the ME who'd worked Katrina McGuire's murder case that had confirmed their link.

"It's true." Duncan's voice. Flat. Cold. And coming from right behind her.

She pressed her hands against the table. Thanks to the high-end equipment that Pate had stocked in her lab, she'd had the results in just a few hours. Hours that Duncan had spent pacing.

She turned toward him. "Same mother. Same father." A father who'd been a werewolf.

Duncan shook his head. "I don't remember a brother, I don't—"

"You remember his screams. Now that you've seen him again, you'll probably start to remember even more." She walked toward him. Duncan's body was thick with tension and the room seemed charged with his desperate energy. "You were a kid then, too, you—"

"I was five. I would have remembered him. Not just screams. *Him*."

Holly swallowed. "You survived a blood bath. Your mother was slaughtered. You must have been in shock when the authorities found you."

"And I—what? Just pretended my own brother didn't exist?"

"You were a child," she said as she tried to keep her voice soothing. "You can't blame yourself for something that happened back then."

"He blames me. He hates me."

Connor certainly seemed to. "Well, if Pate's intel on him is right, the guy is psychotic so he probably blames a lot of people for—"

Duncan's head had snapped up.

*I said the wrong thing. Oh, crap.*

"He's slaughtered so many. He's *my* blood, that's what your test showed, right? That's what he told me." Duncan sucked in a deep breath. "A killer...that's what he is."

"But that's *not* what you are." She wanted to shake him—so she did. A hard yank against his shoulders. So much for soothing. "You aren't him. You haven't spent years killing. You're a good agent. A good man. Whatever he is, that isn't you."

"But we share blood. A father." His brows furrowed. "Wait, if my father was a werewolf, was it some kind pack war? Is that what happened? Other wolves came and killed him and my mother?"

And here was going to be another revelation that wasn't easy to give. "I...I got the ME from your hometown to fax me the autopsy reports for your parents."

"What?"

"I should have told you first but..." But what if she'd been wrong? "Duncan, the man who died, he *wasn't* your father."

But Duncan shook his head. "He was. That was my family. My mother. My father. My—"

"Do you remember them? Or do you just remember..." She hated hurting him. "Do you just remember that the cops told you that your parents were dead?"

His silence was her answer.

"You don't remember your life with them, do you?"

His jaw locked. "I don't remember anything before the blood and screams."

He was ripping out her heart. She couldn't stand for him to be in pain. "You were alone with their bodies for...for three days."

His pupils expanded, turning his blue eyes almost totally black. No trace of gold showed in his eyes.

"The ME...he told me that one of the cops found you in the closet. You were covered in blood. The woman in the house—"

"*My mother.*"

The pain in his voice made her ache. "Her body was found outside of the closet. It appeared as if she'd locked you in, and then she'd been killed outside of the door." The ME's reports had said that her blood had slid under the crack near the bottom of the closet door.

Duncan had been trapped in that darkness as the blood came toward him.

All alone.

Three days.

She blinked away the tears in her eyes. She wasn't shaking him now. Just holding him and wishing that she could take all of his pain away.

"How do you know he wasn't my father?"

"Duncan, you know what happens when a werewolf dies in human form."

"The teeth and claws come out."

Because at death, it was if the beast inside was dying, too. The body shifted back to human form, but the beast didn't totally vanish. The claws and teeth always stayed out in death. "I saw...I saw the pictures taken at the scene. The man who died then didn't have claws. There were no fangs either." MEs had been covering up those little telltale signs for years, and she'd even taken the step of calling the retired ME, Louis Hall, to make sure that her suspicions were correct.

*"Hell, no, lady,"* he'd told her, voice grousing with age. *"I know a werewolf when I see one. Had two of 'em cross my table. Scared the hell out of me at first. That slaughter? No, those were two humans who died."*

Darkness had filled Duncan's gaze. The same deep rage that had burned from Connor's eyes.

"He knows what happened to them," Duncan muttered.

Yes, she suspected that Connor knew a great deal.

"I'm going to make him tell me." He spun away from her and rushed for the doors.

But those doors were already swinging open. Pate stood there. With Shane and Elias at his back.

"Duncan." Pate's gaze swept over him. "I'm going to need you to come with us."

"Get out of my way, Pate," Duncan snapped. His hands were at his sides. His claws? Most definitely out.

Pate shook his head. "Don't make us do this the hard way."

Duncan laughed. "Like there's any other way now." He pointed toward the doors. "That asshole in Containment Five knows about—"

"You mean your brother? The alpha werewolf who's been clawing his way through the town? That asshole?"

She could have slugged Pate right then. Holly marched toward him. "You tapped into my computer."

He nodded. "And your phone line."

Jerk. She should have known he'd pull tricks like that.

But Pate's stare actually seemed to hold real sympathy as it turned back to Duncan. "In the morning, I'll let you grill Connor as long as you want. But the moon is going to start rising soon. Your first full moon. And I can't take chances with this night."

"Scared I'll hurt you?"

"No, scared you'll hurt *her*." Pate's attention shifted to Holly, then back to Duncan. "The wolf will be in control. What do you think he's gonna want most?"

"Not me," Holly said. That had all the guys looking at her. She licked her lips. "Blood. Revenge." That was what she'd seen in Duncan's eyes.

"I want to talk to Connor." Duncan's voice had deepened. Roughened. Goosebumps rose on her arms.

"In the morning. When the moon is down, and your control is one hundred percent set." Pate's mouth firmed. "I have to make sure you control your beast tonight, and that he doesn't control you. Duncan, you know the first full moon transformation is supposed to be hardest."

"The one that tells me if I stay sane?" Duncan's voice made the chill she felt even worse. "Or proves that I'll be psychotic, just like my brother?"

She so wished she'd never used that word. "Duncan..."

His head inclined toward her. She could see his fangs. So what? She had fangs of her own. Holly reached for his hand. "You can talk to him tomorrow."

There were no transfer orders on Connor yet. Duncan would get his answers. They had time.

"Just come with us for tonight," Pate directed. "We've got a secure cell waiting for you."

"Like the last one?" Duncan mocked. "I ripped right through those bars."

Pate's cheeks flushed. It looked like Shane fought a smile. Elias...he paled.

"You're going in the holding room tonight."

The holding room? She sucked in a sharp breath. The holding room was the paranormal equivalent of solitary confinement. No windows. Walls reinforced with a combination of silver and steel. One door. Thick. Heavy. An eight by twelve foot prison.

There was only one light that shone from the ceiling in the middle of that room. It was normally where the most dangerous paranormals were kept before transfer. Where Connor probably would have been housed, if Pate hadn't been so worried about Duncan's transformation under the full moon.

Holly's whole body was tight with tension. "That's a little extreme, don't you think?" She didn't want Duncan locked up. The collar was bad enough. "He's one of ours."

"That's why I'm doing everything I can to keep him safe and to keep him from hurting anyone else." Pate rolled his shoulders. "How do you think he'll feel, Hol, if he wakes up tomorrow and finds the dead bodies of his fellow agents around him?"

"That's not—" Holly began.

"It could happen," Duncan said at the same time.

No, it couldn't. Why did she have more faith in Duncan than he did in himself?

Her hold tightened on him. "You're not like that." *Not like Connor.*

"It's time to find out if I am." He pulled away from her. Damn him, he pulled away. Then he glanced back at Pate. "Take me to holding."

"No!" Holly sprang between the men. "He's wearing the collar. Just let him stay here. I can keep an eye on him tonight, I can—"

Duncan's hands closed around her shoulders. He turned her toward him. Kissed her.

Not a hard kiss.

Not wild.

Not what she'd expected.

Soft. Controlled.

*He has control.*

"I won't hurt you," he said.

No, he wouldn't. That was what she was trying to make them all understand. If the idiots would just listen to her.

"Stay away from me tonight," he said as his gaze held hers. "Connor might have set this in motion, but I'll be damned if I lose what matters most to me."

Her heart slammed into her chest. Wait. Was he saying that she mattered? That it wasn't just sex and need?

But then he was pushing her behind him. Heading away with Pate. And Pate was glancing back over his shoulder and giving her a hard glare. "Shane," Pate ordered, "make sure that Holly gets home safely tonight."

The home that still sported a broken window? That reeked of safety.

"Make sure she doesn't go near holding," Pate added.

Shane gave a little salute and sauntered toward her. "Guess we'll be getting cozy tonight."

Duncan froze. Then he turned and gave Shane a glare that would have singed most men. "You fucking won't."

Shane gulped. "Uh, right...I meant..." He straightened quickly. "I'll keep her safe, promise."

Duncan held his gaze. "You'd better."

Then Duncan was gone. Pate was gone. Elias hurried after them.

Holly found that she couldn't move.

"He'll be okay," Shane said, voice soft.

Her gaze cut toward him. Shane could play the carefree card pretty well. He'd done it plenty of times, but she knew there was a whole lot more going on beneath his surface. He had his share of deadly secrets, too. Most of the agents in the Para Unit did. It took a certain type to hunt monsters.

"He's strong. If any man can hold back a beast, it's him." Shane exhaled on a rough sigh. "You get your gear together, and when you're ready to go, you just tell me."

Holly shook her head. "I'm not leaving."

Shane winced. "How did I know you'd say that? Shit, does this mean we'll both be bunking down in the lab tonight? Because those gurneys make for crappy beds."

She wouldn't be bunking anywhere. She'd be keeping an eye on Duncan.

"What is it with you?" Shane asked as he came a bit closer to her. "Shouldn't you hate him...you know...seeing as what you are?"

That had her gaze flying right back to his.

"Your secret's out," he murmured. Then he tapped his teeth. "And when Duncan kissed you a minute ago, your fangs came out, too."

Horrified, she slapped a hand over her mouth. She hadn't even felt the burn of her teeth. How had that happened? She'd been so careful, for so long.

"Don't worry," Shane assured her. "You're not my first vamp. I figure if you haven't gone for my throat by now, you aren't going to."

She shook her head. "I-I'm not." Her fangs had come out. The karahydrelene definitely wasn't in her system any longer. If it was, her fangs would have stayed in check. Without the drug, she'd have to learn normal control—well, normal vampire control, or she'd give herself away to more than just Shane.

His gaze searched hers. "How long ago did you change?"

"It's been a year." It felt like so much longer.

"Is that why you're here?" His hand lifted and waved around the room. "Hiding with the monsters?"

"The prisoners are—"

He laughed, a rough sound that she wouldn't have expected from him. "Who says I'm talking about the prisoners?"

She could only stare at him in surprise.

"The agents...why do you think we're taking the cases?" He stalked toward her, closing in. "You should look beneath the surface more often, Dr. Young."

His eyes...the color seemed to deepen as she gazed at him.

She also realized that his southern accent— the South Carolina drawl that sometimes dipped beneath his words—was gone.

And then he flashed his own fangs.

Startled, no, *terrified,* Holly jumped back. She opened her mouth to scream, but had no chance. Shane had shoved his hand over her lips.

"Now why would you want to do that?" Shane whispered. "I would have thought that you'd be thrilled to find yourself with one of your own."

His right hand was over her mouth. His left wrapped around her body and pulled her close against him.

His body was strong. Powerful. And his teeth...those were the fangs of a vampire.

*One of your own.*

She swallowed back the lump of fear and stared up at the vampire who'd worked beside her for months.

\*\*\*

Duncan marched into the holding room. The lone light shone down from above. Bright. Stark.

"It's just for the night," Pate said from behind him.

Duncan looked back at him. "Unless I go crazy..." *Psychotic.* That had been Holly's word.

Pate waved away Elias. The other agent's face tensed, but, with one last, regretful glance at Duncan, he eased away. Pate waited until that agent had vanished, then he said, "Do you feel the wolf inside?"

Yes. Clawing to get out. Duncan nodded.

"When you were a wolf before, did the man inside have control, or was it the beast that ruled?"

"The man." He'd still been there, no, *he'd* been the beast. They hadn't been separate.

Maybe they never had been.

*My brother.* If his brother was a werewolf, if his father had been, then didn't that mean the beast had been in him the entire time? "I am the wolf," he muttered, clenching his teeth.

"And what does the wolf want?" Pate's question was careful, emotionless.

Duncan realized he was staring at his clenched hands. He looked up and saw Pate staring back at him with hard eyes.

"Do you want revenge? Blood?" Pate demanded as he stepped closer. "Or do you want *her*?"

He wanted it all. "Connor will tell me about my family."

"You sure you want to know? Maybe some things are better left in the dark. Knowing that your brother has been killing for years, with no remorse—"

"Do you think I'm like him?" Duncan cut through his words. His muscles had tightened.

"I think you're a dangerous man," Pate replied softly. "But I knew that about you the moment we met." Pate turned away. "Let's see what the night brings. We'll both find out just how dangerous you can become."

Suspicion had filled Duncan's heart. With the news of Connor, well, his whole life had changed. He wasn't sure what to believe now. Who to believe. "You should have told me," Duncan snapped. The whole time that he'd been in the Para Unit, he'd been a ticking time bomb. Just waiting to get bitten.

"What would have been the point?" Pate asked. "Werewolves walk the earth. You could have been bitten at any moment, heading to the store or even going to a bar." Pate shrugged. "You knew we were battling paranormals. The choice to join the group was *yours*."

The silver burned against his neck. "Did you want me to change?" The question that mattered most. No, the question that mattered most was...*did you set me up to change*?

Because he was realizing that Pate would go to almost any extreme in order to get what he wanted.

"Having a werewolf on my team would be an advantage," Pate said as he gave a faint nod.

The sonofabitch wasn't even acting like the loss of Duncan's humanity was a big deal. Shit.

"But there are other werewolves out there who could have joined the unit. Fully transformed werewolves who *aren't* psychotic." Pate lifted one brow. "So no, I didn't throw one of my own men—"

"To the wolves?" Duncan finished.

"Just so I could up my paranormal power scale for hunting." His lips twisted into a dark smile. "Trust me, I've already got plenty of paranormal power in the unit."

Was he talking about Holly? Or someone else?

The answer was in Pate's eyes. *Someone else.*

"The monsters aren't always the enemy," Pate said as he turned away once more. "Sometimes, they're the men fighting right beside you." Then he was gone. Locking the door.

Sealing Duncan inside the room.

The light shone down from overhead.

Duncan exhaled slowly and tried to remember a time before monsters. A time when he'd had a brother.

A family.

A life.

But it had all been washed away in a tide of rising blood.

\*\*\*

"Seriously, if you keep looking at me like that, I might bite you just for the hell of it," Shane said as his gaze narrowed on her. "Don't tempt me."

She blinked.

"I'm not going for your throat. I had plenty of opportunities." He tilted his head to study her. "Of course, we are all alone now. The others are far away, and I bet you'd never even have the chance to scream."

She shoved him away. Actually, she threw him away. Shane flew back about five feet and crashed into her instrument tray.

He laughed as he rose. His dark, rumbling laughter made goosebumps rise on her arms.

She glanced around desperately, looking for something *wooden*. But when Pate had made her lab, he'd been sure to keep the wood to a minimum. In case anyone found out the truth about her, he hadn't wanted them going all stake crazy.

"I do like a woman with bite." Shane took a step toward her.

Holly flashed her fangs at him. "Take another step, and you'll find out just how much bite I have."

He didn't take another step. He just—appeared right in front of her. She blinked, and he was there. Then he grabbed her arms. Held her tight. "You are just a beginner in my world."

Dark. Deep. The easy going mask was totally gone, and she stared up into his eyes, seeing the darkness that she'd always sensed with him.

"A vampire's power comes with age. Your *bite* can never compare to mine."

In his gaze, she saw the cold promise of death. "Wh-what do you want?"

His hold eased. "To keep you safe." He pulled in a breath. His fangs receded. His stare started to look a bit less like the grim reaper's. "That is my job, isn't it? What Pate told me to do?"

"Does Pate know about you?" He couldn't. No way. He—

"Of course. Why do you think he recruited me?" His tongue ran over the edge of his teeth, as if checking to make sure the fangs were gone. "If you're going after monsters, doesn't it make sense to have your own paranormal arsenal to fight them?"

Her heart thudded too hard in her chest.

"But what I don't understand is why Pate isn't using you more. Why keep you here, locked away, when you could be fighting in the night with us?"

"B-because he wants me to find a cure. He wants me to be human again."

"There *is* no cure for us."

"Not yet." Her chin lifted. "But I'm working on it. Vampirism is a virus. We were created. We can be cured."

"Is that Pate talking or you?"

"I—"

"What if we don't want to be *cured*?"

That was the question she'd hoped he wouldn't ask. In the back of her mind, she'd wondered if Pate wanted to completely eradicate all of the vampires by *making* them human again. No choices. Just a cure.

"Pate was holding back on me." Anger beat in Shane's words.

Now she was the one to grab him. Her fingers locked around his arms, and she forgot her fear. "Wouldn't you go back, if you could?"

"Hell, no," he said with absolute certainty. "Why do that? I've got more power than most can ever imagine. I don't age. I don't die. I can control any human I want. I'm not decomposing in a grave. I'm not—"

"But everyone around you will die. All of those you love." Her fear.

A muscle jerked in his jaw. "When I find someone to love, you can bet that I *won't* let her die."

There was a cold promise in his words.

She believed that promise. "What if she doesn't want to live forever?"

He didn't speak.

Maybe he didn't have an answer for that question.

"Look, Shane, I need—"

The lights flickered over them. Flickered, then flashed off as the room sank into darkness.

She jerked away from Shane.

"What the hell?" His footsteps shuffled away from her.

"The generator will switch on," she assured him, fumbling as she made her way to the desk. Vampires didn't have enhanced vision like werewolves. They couldn't see in the dark. Unfortunately. Vampires were physically strongest during the time when their vision was weakest.

When the sun rose, their strength depleted. That was why she tried to sleep during the day and spend all of her late nights in her lab.

From a few feet away, Shane swore. She heard a bang, as if he'd run into something.

Seconds ticked by, and the generator didn't come back on.

It should have come back on. Protocol was that the generator automatically took over power control in five seconds.

It had been thirty seconds. She'd counted every second.

"It's not coming on," he muttered. He was farther away now, a good ten feet by the sound of things.

Then, before she could speak, Holly heard a howl. A long, angry howl that seemed to shake the building.

"Connor said that Duncan would lose everything," she whispered. And Connor's pack of wolves had attacked the facility before. Were they doing it again?

She rushed for the door. Rushed for Duncan.

But found herself caught in Shane's tight grip.

\*\*\*

The lone light in the room shut off. The darkness came, surrounding him. Duncan lunged forward instinctively. His hands slammed into the wall. The silver burned him, and he yanked back his hands.

He remembered another time. Another place.

More darkness.

More walls that held him inside.

Only then...then there had been blood, too. The wet blood that had slid under the door.

*Help me! Duncan!*

He'd heard that cry, but hadn't been able to help.

Because...

His hands lifted again. Slammed into the door. His eyes had adjusted to the darkness, adjusted so quickly, and he could see clearly now. When he'd been blinded before...

*I couldn't help because I was already in the closet. She locked me in.*

The screams for help had been coming from outside of the closet. From outside, where his mother had been dead.

Where his brother had watched her die?

A howl echoed from deep in the facility. Long, angry.

The beast in him wanted to respond.

He wanted out of that room.

Out of the darkness.

His fists pounded into the door. The silver burned, but he kept pounding. Kept pounding.

*Help me!* The scream that he could still hear.

The door wasn't giving. The collar around his neck fucking burned.

*Collared. Like an animal.*

Because he was.

The silver bit into his skin, burned hotter as if...as if someone had increased the intensity.

His hands rose to his neck. Clawed against the collar. The silver *was* hotter, and the collar was tightening around him.

Now he knew why the other wolf had howled.

Duncan was crying out, too, screaming and howling in fury.

Because some bastard was torturing him in the dark. And that torture, it drove the man back, even as the beast clawed for his freedom.

# CHAPTER NINE

"Let me go!" Holly yelled as she fought against Shane.

"I'm supposed to keep you safe!"

But there were more howls now. And those cries...they didn't sound like the beasts were attacking.

It sounded as if the beasts were being attacked.

"They're hurting!" Holly told him. "Duncan could be in trouble!"

"And you have to save him?"

"Yes, I do." She kicked him as hard as she could. Considering her vamp strength, it was pretty damn hard. "Now let me...*go!*" She head-butted him.

He barely grunted, and his hold just tightened. "Werewolves can see in the dark. The moon is full tonight. They'll be at full strength—"

More howls. More pain. More suffering.

He had to hear their agony. "Don't you get it? Someone is hurting them!"

"Like the collars they wear don't hurt?" His cold tone mocked her. "What do you think has been happening during all of their containment time?"

"The collars don't make them scream like that, not unless..." she broke off, then whispered, "not unless someone has increased the intensity of the silver."

"Someone who hated the wolves? Bet we got a long list of folks like that at the facility. Especially after the last attack when so many human guards died."

Someone could want payback. Revenge.

She wrenched free. Stumbled back to her desk. Holly found the collar remote that she had locked in her top drawer. "If you won't let me leave this room alone, then you take me to Duncan."

"Now that's a better plan." Then his hand was on her elbow as he steered her out of the med unit and through the hallway. With every step, the howls become louder. But even though the howls were wild and desperate in their intensity, they were the only sounds that she heard. There were no shouts from the agents and guards who should have been on duty that night. No rushing footsteps as people went to check on the prisoners.

What the hell?

Just howls. So many howls.

*Duncan, hold on.*

Because she knew he was trapped in that darkness. Trapped as he'd been before, when he'd been just a child.

When he'd waited for death to come for him.

\*\*\*

Pate ran from his office when he heard the howls. "Guards!" he bellowed. Something was wrong. The power never went off at this facility, and he could tell by their cries that the wolves were in pain.

No one answered his call.

He yanked his weapon out of its holster. He knew this facility like the back of his hand. No need for lights. He rushed down the hallway, heading first for Holly because he had to make sure his sister was alive and—

"I knew you'd go for her first." The voice, low and familiar, came from the dark corridor to his right.

Pate spun around, but he moved too slowly. A blast echoed around him even as a bullet drove into his chest.

Pate hit the floor. He squeezed his fingers around the trigger of his weapon and managed to fire, but he didn't know if the bullet found its target. So he fired again. Again.

He fired until his gun clicked and the chamber was empty.

\*\*\*

The gunshots froze Holly in the hallway. Then the scent hit her. *Blood.*

Shane stiffened. "That's not fucking good."

They were almost to the holding room. So close. And she could hear Duncan's howls.

"You can follow the blood scent," she said, her hands clenching in the fabric of Shane's shirt. "Go—find out what's happening!"

"I'm not leaving you on your own."

There were no more gunshots. Just howls. Pain-filled howls erupting from Duncan's room. "I'm not on my own," she told him. "I'll be with Duncan."

"Yeah, that's the problem. Do you *hear* that guy? You go in there, and he'll rip you apart."

"No, he won't." Holly said the words with absolute certainty. She trusted Duncan.

The room's keypad was to her right. She knew the exact position of the numbers on the pad, so she typed in the code for the door quickly, then swiped her thumb over the lock. Luckily, the security there was wired through a separate system not the building's main power supply.

The heavy door opened with a hiss.

"Follow the blood scent!" Holly ordered as she stepped into the room. "Go!"

Before he could speak, another growl sounded.

Holly looked across the room.

In the back corner, she saw the glow of silver. The collar. And it should *never* be glowing so brightly like that. That heavy glow meant the collar was burning at full intensity. A kill level. She fumbled, trying to input the necessary code into the collar's remote. She typed in the override code that she'd created to disconnect the collar. To free Duncan.

Only...only the remote wasn't working. She typed the code again and again, but—*nothing*.

The only reason that code wouldn't work? Someone had reset the system.

Someone was trying to kill Duncan. Trying to kill all of the werewolves in the facility.

*Payback.*

Her gaze lifted from the glowing silver around Duncan's neck, and she saw that his eyes—his eyes were glowing, too. Glowing with the power of his beast.

"Hol...ly..." More a growl than her name.

She licked lips gone too dry. Her fangs had started to burn in her mouth. Probably due to the fear that wanted to rise in her.

*I won't fear him.*

Shane came up behind her. *So much for him following the blood scent.* "What the hell is happening with his collar?"

"I think someone got in the system. The wolves are all howling because they're hurting. The collars are set on full intensity." She could feel Shane behind her. "If we don't get the intensity lowered soon, they'll die."

"Turn his off!"

Duncan's growls were worse. His eyes glowing even brighter.

"I can't," she said as hurried toward Duncan. "I *can't*!"

Shane grabbed her and pulled her back.

Duncan stopped growling. Stopped howling.

His eyes stared right at her and Shane.

"I don't..." Her words came in a weak whisper. "I don't think you should be touching me." Because in that darkness, she could see the full fury of Duncan's stare.

"And I'm not letting him touch you," Shane said as his grip tightened around her. "I told Pate

I'd keep you safe. I damn well will. That collar isn't gonna let him attack me—"

A snap came from the back corner. Like a bone breaking or—or a collar breaking. *Being ripped apart.* Because the collar wasn't glowing around Duncan's neck anymore. Two glowing chunks of silver were on the floor now.

"Ah, damn," Shane rasped. "This is gonna hurt."

Duncan's glowing eyes were locked on him. Then Duncan was coming for Shane. Rushing forward. There was a thud as their bodies hit. They slammed into the floor. The scent of blood rose from the men, and Holly didn't know which one was hurt.

The werewolf?

The vampire?

Her own fangs were out, and she wasn't just going to *stand there* while they battled in front of her. These guys, they were the good guys, weren't they?

*Yes.*

At least, Duncan was. She'd figure Shane out later.

So Holly yelled, "Stop!"

For an instant, they did.

Then they went right back to fighting. So she reached down and wrapped her arms around a body—a body with broad shoulders and a scent that had started to haunt her.

Duncan turned at once, and his arms curled around her, holding her tight. She could feel the rage vibrating in his body, but his hold on her was controlled, so careful.

"You shouldn't...be here..." Duncan growled.

"This is exactly where I need to be."

"The moon..."

"It's not all the way up yet." Not yet. But close. They were running out of time. "So instead of you and Shane trying to beat the crap out of each other, let's go find out who's trying to kill the werewolves."

His eyes widened. "The wolves?" Then his head jerked up, as if he'd just heard their cries.

"They're howling. They're hurting." Her nails bit into his arms. "You're an alpha. An alpha takes care of the others." *Your brother is out there.*

He shuddered, then rasped, "Help...them..."

That was what they had to do.

"Uh, you sure about this?" Shane muttered. "His collar is *gone.*"

And the moon was rising. Yes, she got it. But they didn't have any options.

"Take us to the wolves," Holly said.

Duncan's fingers laced with hers. He ran from the room, pulling her with him. Shane rushed behind them.

Holly inhaled. There was more blood. So much more. Coming from all around them. Her fangs were out, fully extended, and her body was held on a razor's edge of tension.

"*Pate...*" Her whisper. Duncan was heading after his brother, and she was worried about her own.

"Pate knows how to take care of himself," Shane said from behind her.

Pate was strong, resourceful, but he was still just a man. In a building full of howling werewolves and at least two vampires.

"We'll find him," Shane told her, "just follow your werewolf first, okay? I don't think he can hold it together much longer."

Duncan's hold had tightened around her fingers. He was pretty much dragging her behind him. She rushed to keep up. As they headed through the darkness, the howls began to die away. One. A second. A third.

At first, those howls had chilled her, but for them to just stop...*are the wolves dead*?

Then Duncan was snarling and breaking away from her. He ran forward into the darkness. "Duncan!" Holly yelled after him and blindly raced straight ahead.

Metal shrieked. Bent.

Shane swore.

Then—then there was a faint glint of light. A hum broke the air and the generator *finally* switched on.

The backup lights were fainter as the power ran low, but Holly was so happy to be able to see again that she wasn't about to complain. Her legs pumped faster as she ran.

The door to Containment Area Five had been busted down, courtesy of Duncan. He was inside that room now. She could hear his snarls and also hear—

"*Stop!*"

That voice—Elias?

She hurried into the room. Saw that Connor was still in his cell, but he was on the floor, lying facedown. He didn't even seem to be breathing.

Duncan was on the other side of the area, and he had knocked Elias off his feet. As she stared in horror, Holly saw Duncan's hands—his *claws*—go for Elias's throat.

"Stop!" Elias yelled. "Dammit, Duncan, it's me! Don't!"

But those claws were inches away from the agent's throat. Holly leapt across the room and tried to wrench him away from Elias. "Don't attack him!"

Too late. His claws slashed across Elias's neck even as Holly and Shane yanked Duncan back.

The scent of the blood flooded through Holly's nostrils.

"Kill..." Duncan growled and he fought against her and Shane. Duncan slung Shane across the room, and the vampire rammed into the side of Connor's cell.

Then Duncan's hands wrapped around Holly's shoulders. Her eyes widened as she stared up at him. His gaze glowed so brightly that the sight of it stole her breath.

"Duncan?" Holly whispered. "That's Elias you're attacking. He's on our side." Elias wasn't armed. Didn't have any weapon at all that she could see.

He wasn't trying to fight back. He just huddled on the floor, with his hand over his throat. His eyes were on Duncan, and, there was no mistaking the horror in his gaze.

"*Kill...*" Duncan snarled again, and he tried to toss her aside.

She wasn't in the mood to be tossed. So she stared right back into his too-bright eyes. Stared as hard as she could and said, "*Stop.*" She was using her vampire control, the power that she'd never wanted to exert over him, but she couldn't let him kill another agent. This wasn't Duncan.

This was the beast.

The glow of his eyes burned even brighter as he stiffened. But he didn't move. Didn't try to rush toward Elias.

"Wh-what's happening?" Elias demanded.

The claws hadn't sliced him too deeply or he wouldn't be speaking. Good. They were lucky. If she and Shane hadn't both been pulling Duncan back, he could have slashed the agent's throat wide open.

"Someone took over the controls on the collars." *Someone got into our computer system. Disabled the main power, generator, and monitors. And that someone tried to kill the wolves.*

Duncan's hands were still wrapped around her wrists. She could feel the edge of his claws. "Is your control back?" Holly asked him carefully.

He just stared at her. Glared at her.

"I'll take that as a no." Crap. An alarm started to sound, a high-pitched wail. But the wolves didn't start howling again.

Connor wasn't moving at all, but above the scent of Elias's blood, Holly could smell the acrid odor of...burned flesh.

"Stay here," Holly whispered to Duncan, pushing with her compulsion, then she eased away from him. Shane was at her side instantly, shadowing her.

She pointed toward Elias. "Can you help him?" *Without taking a bite?*

His lips tightened. "Newborn," he whispered for her ears alone, "I know how to stay in control."

She hoped so.

Holly made short work of opening Connor's cell. She glanced over at Duncan. He watched her with his wild gaze, but he didn't move.

*Couldn't move?*

The power of compulsion was a dangerous thing. It would be so easy to misuse. She knew plenty of vampires had misused their power to torture and kill, that was why many of them were housed in Purgatory.

"Wh-why isn't Duncan attacking?" Elias asked. Holly glanced over and saw him pushing to his feet.

"Because she's not letting him," Shane said without looking away from Duncan. Ah, he knew exactly where the threat was. Like her, he must wonder just how long that control would last over Duncan.

She crept into the cell.

"That's a bad idea," Shane called out. "Don't get too close to the beast!"

"I'm a doctor." Holly took another tentative step forward. "I can't just let someone die in front of me." She knew that with every passing second, the moon was rising higher in the sky. When the moon reached its zenith, that was when the wolf would be at his strongest.

Connor didn't move as she eased toward him. The silver had definitely burned him. She could see the faint tendrils of smoke still rising from the collar. Unlike Duncan, Connor hadn't been strong enough to break the collar.

"Who did this?" Holly whispered. Then, louder, "Shane, you need to check the other wolves!"

"Th-that's why I came in..." Elias said, voice breaking. "I heard his...howls..."

She could hear no sounds at all coming from Connor. He didn't seem to be breathing. Holly's fingers slipped toward the silver collar, toward his neck—

And, in an instant, he was on his feet. On his feet, with one arm locked around her and with his claws at her throat. "You should have stayed back." His body trembled against hers, but his hold was incredibly strong.

She tried to yank away from him, but his claws cut over her skin. The wet warmth of her blood trickled down her neck.

"I thought the FBI wasn't supposed...to be...in for torture..." The arm around her waist tightened. "Guess it doesn't count...when it's just against...the animals?"

She tried to press back against him, attempting to move her neck away from his claws. "I didn't do this! I'm here to help you!"

"Bullshit." He turned her body, positioning them so that they stared through the cell's bars— and right at a silent Duncan. "You wanted him to be top dog in this town, so you were getting rid of the competition."

She tried to shake her head. When she felt the slice of claws on her skin, Holly froze. "I don't— don't care about who is alpha..."

His head bent toward hers. "You should," he whispered. "Because only the alpha will be able to save you."

*"Let...her...go..."* Duncan's order. Growled. Barely human.

"Come make me," Connor taunted.

Duncan didn't move.

Because she'd told him to stay back? Her stupid compulsion?

Now Connor was the one to growl. "Vampire. I know what you did." She felt the angry rumble behind her. "You think he's your...dog...on a leash?"

She shook her head. No, she hadn't thought that. She'd just been trying to stop Duncan from killing Elias.

Connor spun her around. Yanked her up on her toes. Glared down at her. And that was when she realized that his collar wasn't glowing anymore. Not at all. *Deactivated.* There was nothing to hold him back now.

"You don't control us," he snapped at her. "We destroy you." Then he lifted his hand, and she knew he was going to cut open her throat. Maybe even take her head.

That would sure teach her to play good Samaritan.

Since she wasn't in the mood to lose her head. Holly slammed into him with all of her might. She kicked and punched with her vampire strength. He stumbled back, just a few steps, and she used that opportunity to race for the entrance to his cell.

"Duncan!" Holly yelled. "Help me!"

And he was there. Bellowing his fury. Pulling her against him, holding her tight. Shane was right behind him, with fangs glinting.

"Mine," Duncan roared as he pushed her behind him. "You don't hurt...*mine*."

A little late for that part. Her throbbing neck told her that, yes, she'd most definitely been hurt.

But then bones began to snap. Duncan was shifting. Connor was shifting. Their bones popped and bent. Reshaped. Fur exploded along their bodies.

"We need to get out of here," Shane snarled. "*Now*." Then he was hauling her out of striking distance. Once she was clear of the cell, Shame slammed the door closed. The wolves were locked inside.

And they *were* wolves now. Fully transformed. Fully beasts. Completely pissed off as they faced each other.

Brothers shouldn't battle like this. "No," Holly cried. "We need to get Duncan out of there."

Shane caught her hands. "His wolf needs to prove he's alpha, or you're a dead woman."

"I'm a vampire, I'm already dead." Wasn't that the way the story went? But Duncan wasn't dead. "He needs—"

The wolves were attacking each other. Claws were flashing, snarls filled the air, and the scent of blood deepened.

Duncan was about to kill his own brother, and even if Connor was a psychotic asshole, she couldn't let Duncan carry this weight on his shoulders. She leapt forward and yanked open the cell door.

Shane shoved it closed again in an instant.

She shoved *him*. "Okay, you're older than me, stronger, but you will not stop me from helping Duncan! He needs me!" She pointed toward the door. "You're an agent—where are all the humans? Why are the wolves so quiet? Go help *them*." Her chin lifted. "And leave Duncan to me."

A muscle flexed in his jaw. But he knew something was wrong in the facility, just as she did.

"Are you going to let them all die?" Holly pushed.

The answer was on his face. No, he wasn't. "Don't get yourself killed," he ordered, then he ran from the room.

"I can't make that promise," she whispered.

Elias scrambled out after Shane.

And she opened the cell door and prepared to walk between two werewolves.

*** 

Leaving a woman on her own with two snarling werewolves wasn't exactly the way Shane would normally operate.

But the situation wasn't normal.

Pate should have come to find them by now. The guy hadn't showed, and there was only one reason why Pate wouldn't be searching for his little sister.

*Because he's dead.*

Shane inhaled deeply. He caught the scent of blood and ran faster.

*Or close to dead.*

He'd heard a gunshot before. Two blasts. The wolves in that place would be fighting with fangs and claws, but any humans there—like Pate—would be using guns.

Shane whirled around a corner. He'd headed back toward Holly's lab. He took another turn and—

Saw Pate's body slumped in the hallway. A thick pool of blood was around him. Hell, *no*.

He sank to his knees beside Pate. The director's breath rasped out, weak, and Pate groaned when Shane touched him.

*Too much blood.*

Humans weren't equipped to survive this kind of attack.

It was a good thing that Pate wasn't exactly human. Shane bit his wrist and forced his blood into Pate's mouth. Pate's eyelids flickered, but he took the blood. The guy knew better than to fight in a situation like this.

Shave would give him a little more blood, get Pate to tell him what the hell had happened and—

He heard the faint rustle of a footstep behind him. "I knew you weren't human."

*Fuck.*

He lunged up and whirled to face the threat.

But a wooden bullet sank into his chest.

# CHAPTER TEN

"Stop fighting!" Holly yelled.

And Holly's blood...the scent was around him. Driving him insane. The bastard before him had dared to use his claws against her skin. He'd cut her. Would have killed her.

Duncan swiped his claws over the back of the other wolf.

A wolf that was big, muscled, with dark black fur. A wolf that looked just like his own altered form, except for his eyes.

Connor leapt back.

Duncan's muscles tightened as he prepared to lunge for the wolf again.

Only Holly jumped between them. "*Stop!*" Fury hardened her voice. "Don't you realize that someone is hunting us all? Connor, you weren't the only one attacked tonight. Duncan was, too."

Attacked. Locked in the dark. Locked in a prison too like the one that haunted his past.

And then the silver had started to burn him.

The silver collar still circled Connor's neck, but the silver didn't glow. Connor paced near the back of the cell, never taking his eyes off Duncan.

Duncan stalked forward. His body bumped into Holly. *Move back.*

He didn't want her to watch this battle. She already saw him as enough of an animal, but he couldn't let the threat to her continue.

Then he heard the crack of thunder. No, not thunder, a shot. He saw the jerk of Connor's head and knew that his brother had heard the sound, too.

*I came in here to save him.* He'd heard Connor's cries, and his instinct had been to protect. But then Connor had turned on Holly. On him.

As he always would. Holly had been right. Connor was psychotic.

*Am I?*

"Someone else is hunting," Holly said. Her fingers sank into the fur on Duncan's back. "Please, we have to go help the others. We can't stay here." Her breath rushed out. "And I can't let you kill your own brother."

Why not? His brother had made it clear that Duncan was on his hit list.

"Duncan? Are you in there?" Then she dropped to her knees. Brought herself too close to his fangs. That scent—her blood—had him snarling. "Control your wolf. Help me."

He couldn't pull back. There was no changing into a man now. The beast was in power, and Duncan didn't even know how to go back from this point.

But...but he could still help her. Carefully, he put his body between hers and Connor's. Then he edged back with her, making sure that he protected her with every step as they headed for the cell door.

One step.

Another.

Connor wasn't following. He was just watching them, with his head cocked to the side.

*He told me that I would lose her. That I would lose everything.*

Duncan wasn't in the mood to lose.

He pushed Holly back through the cell door. Then he followed her. Connor stood inside the cell.

"Come on," Holly said. "We have to find Pate."

Duncan turned away from the cell as Holly locked the door, caging Connor once again. Then he ran with her toward the exit. For every step that she took, he was by her side.

Connor howled after him. The call was a challenge.

Duncan ignored him. Even the wolf that he was knew some things were more important than fighting.

Holly. She was what mattered.

So he ran with her. He followed the scents that flooded his nose. She'd gone with him to find his brother—*a battle that will come again*—and now it was time for him to find Pate.

It didn't take long to find the other man. They went back toward the lab, running quickly, and when Holly saw Pate's prone body sprawled on the floor, a wild cry broke from her.

Then she was diving down beside him. Both Pate and Shane were on that floor. They weren't moving, and there was so much blood around them. Too much.

*A trap.*

A trap that Shane had been caught in as he rushed to Pate's aid.

Duncan spun around, his strong senses picking up the other presence in that hallway. Then he saw the gun. Aimed at Holly.

He rushed at the attacker. A bullet plowed into his body when he jumped into the air, but there was no burn so he knew that the bullet wasn't made of silver. *Your mistake.* The wound didn't slow him down. The shooter fired again, and that bullet missed Duncan entirely.

His claws sank into the shooter's shoulders, and he took the bastard down, just as he'd taken the man down when he'd found him near Connor's cell.

Elias hit the floor with a thud. "I'm doing...what you wanted...*helping you!*"

No, the bastard was killing.

His claws drove deeper into Elias's shoulders.

"It's too late," Elias shouted. Then the alarm finally stopped. Silence. Perfect. Deep.

He could hear Holly's desperate breaths—and the faint hitch that signaled her pain.

Her pain?

His head whipped around. Holly had sagged against the wall. The second bullet. Shit. It had slammed into her.

Her eyes were closed. She slumped to the floor.

A slow hiss slipped from the ceiling. A new scent filled the air. Acrid. Thick.

"Pate had a backup security system in place. Did you know that? Gas...to knock out the paranormals, in case they ever overpowered the humans." The gas was pumping down now. Choking Duncan. He wrenched away from Elias.

"It'll..." Elias heaved out a hard breath. "Knock us...all out...when you wake up...they'll be dead..."

The fuck, *no*. He rushed toward Holly.

"All...dead..." Elias whispered behind him, his own voice slurring. "Then you'll...be next."

No, he wouldn't be. His gaze was locked on Holly. *Not moving*. If the bullet was wooden, then she wouldn't move until he dug it out of her heart—*if* it had hit her heart.

"Maybe...you'll...be now..." Elias rasped.

Duncan spun back to face him. Saw that Elias had that gun of his up again.

*No more.*

The beast took over totally then. He launched at Elias.

Ripped. Bit. Clawed.

And Elias was dead before his head slammed back into the floor.

\*\*\*

She...*hurt*.

Holly tried to open her eyes. She was being pulled—dragged?—by someone, and there was a tight pressure on her shoulder.

Not just pressure. Pain. Like knives were digging into her. She tried to lift her arm and fight her attacker, but she just touched heavy fur.

And she smelled an animal.

Fear had adrenaline pulsing through her. She screamed and sank her fingers into the fur.

A wolf growled at her.

Then she saw his eyes. Those glowing eyes that only belonged to Duncan. The knifes in her shoulder had been his teeth. He'd been dragging her.

They were...outside now. She sucked in fresh air and wondered why her throat burned. Beside her, his body heaved.

She tried to sit up, but couldn't. She was so damn weak that her body just slumped sideways.

She saw the flash of lights in the distance. Cars, rushing toward them. What in the hell was happening?

"Duncan?" She tried to reach for him again, but he backed away from her. "Duncan, change back."

The wolf stared at her.

Her heart beat faster, and she became aware of her other wounds, especially the bullet wound. Elias had *shot* her.

And Pate.

And Shane.

But at least Elias had been a crappy shot. If his bullet had gone into her heart—and it had been a *wooden* bullet—her body would have instantly shut down.

All the better for him to come and take her head.

Her heartbeat shook her chest. "What happened to them? Why are we outside?" Her brother had been so still. She'd tried to help him, but Elias had shot her. Then the air had started to smell funny.

*Gas.*

Duncan was still backing away from her. Still staying in animal form.

Goosebumps rose on her arms. She could hear the sound of footsteps. Pounding toward them. Who was coming? What was happening? She looked straight up and saw that the moon was almost to the zenith point. Oh, no. Oh, *hell, no,* that wasn't good.

"Get away from the woman!" A hard voice shouted.

Her gaze jerked to the left. She recognized the faces of a few of the guards who'd just run toward them. Where had the guards been when all hell broke loose inside the facility? And were these guys on their side...or had they been working with Elias?

Duncan growled at them.

"Werewolf," she heard one of the men say. Wait, that was Brent, one of the newer agents in the unit. She'd patched him up after a particularly bloody mission a few weeks ago. "Dr. Young, don't move!" he ordered. "We'll take him out!" Brent lifted his gun.

He was going to fire at Duncan. "No!" She stumbled toward Duncan and wrapped her arms around the wolf. Duncan's muscles were hard beneath her hands.

"Get away from him!" Brent shouted. "I got the call at home from Elias...I know Duncan's gone rogue. He's killing—and we won't let him kill you!"

Is that what Elias had done? Set Duncan up for murder? Why?

"It's not like that," Holly yelled, refusing to budge. Duncan's throat was vibrating with a growl. With rage. That moon was so close to the zenith. "Just lower your weapons, and I can explain!" There were half a dozen men there and...

"They're dead inside!" A man shouted, running toward them. His voice broke. "All of them...the other agents and guards are all dead. They've been ripped open!"

No. No, that wasn't possible.

*But I smelled the blood.*

Brent stepped toward them. He still had his gun up. "Get away from him, doctor."

"It's *Duncan*!"

"Not right now, it isn't. It's a werewolf. One with blood on his claws and blood staining his fangs."

Because their flashlights were centered on her and Duncan. She knew they both had to look like walking nightmares.

"Dr. Young..." Brent's voice had tightened. "Are those...*fangs* in your mouth?"

No, it was freaking candy. She snapped her teeth together. "Get back." Then she stood fully, trying to shield Duncan with her body. "Drop your guns!"

They all lifted the weapons.

Duncan snarled.

Six weapons. All pointed at her.

All ready to fire. Why? Because she had pointy teeth? Or maybe because she had a werewolf at her side? A werewolf who would *not* be smart and just stay behind her.

"I can explain all of this," she said, and the words were mostly true. She could explain some of this, if she had the chance.

"Don't...fuckin'...aim at my...sister!"

Pate's voice. Pate's wonderful, angry voice. Her shoulders slumped. He was alive. *Yes.* Pate would make everything right again.

"Shoot the...wolf..." Pate continued as he shuffled forward. "Not...her..."

What? "*No!*"

But Duncan had leapt away from her. *So I wouldn't be a target.* And gunfire was erupting. The wolf dodged the bullets and raced away from the men.

She screamed, but the wolf didn't stop. She didn't blame him. Not with bullets chasing him.

Then the men were running after him. And he—he was vanishing into the night.

She wanted to chase after him, too, but her body felt cold and numb and when her knees gave way, she sank to the ground.

"Help her!" Pate barked.

But there was no help for her. Her body was so cold, and Duncan was gone. He'd vanished, and the gunfire was quiet now.

At least he'd gotten away.

But what would happen to him?

"Holly?" She forced her eyes to stay open as she looked up at Pate. Blood covered him. How was he there? She'd seen the bullet wounds to his chest. She knew the damage they'd done. Humans would die from injuries like those.

They wouldn't be walking around minutes later.

"How...long..." Holly whispered.

Brent was there. Lifting her into his arms. "Is she supposed to be this cold?"

"No, she's going to need blood. A lot of it." Pate put his hand on her cheek. "It's okay. I've got you now. You know your kind can't afford this much blood loss."

No, they couldn't. To kill a vampire, you had to either cut off the vamp's head or drain all of the vampire's blood away.

The easy trick for getting the vampire in the position that you *could* do those things? Paralyze the vamp with a wooden bullet.

But in order to paralyze the vampire, the bullet had to go straight into the heart.

Elias had missed her heart, but he'd sure nicked vital organs and made the blood gush from her. She'd tried to stay strong for as long as she could.

But she was too weak now.

"I'll take care of you," Pate promised.

She didn't believe him. And, staring at him then, she didn't trust him, either. She'd risked her life for Pate, died for him, and now, she could only ask, "How long...have you been a-a vampire?"

Because she could see the edge of his fangs.

All emotion drained away from his face. The man she'd known was gone. He stared down at her as a stranger. "Long enough."

She realized that the world she'd known was a total lie.

Then she was being carried away. She couldn't fight. Could barely even lift her hand. Behind her, she heard a wolf howl. But the howl was so far away.

\*\*\*

Holly paced her living room. Again and again. As soon as she'd gotten an infusion of blood—okay, four infusions—she'd run away from Pate.

He'd let her go.

Probably because he knew there was no place she could escape to that he couldn't follow.

Pate...*a vampire*? How had she not known about him? Why hadn't he told her? Had he been a vampire that night, when she'd been so desperate to save him? By that time, had he already been changed? No wonder he was so keen for her to find a cure. The guy must have been using her karahydrelene, too.

Her hand lifted and smoothed over the wound on her chest. Well, not really a wound any longer. It had healed as she ingested the blood.

The Para Unit's containment facility in the woods was being shut down. The order had come from above. The place had been deemed too unsecure and dangerous.

Only one prisoner was still alive in that building—and Connor was due to be immediately transferred to Purgatory. The other wolves—even Saul—had all died from silver poisoning. Their collars had been cranked up to full power.

And as for Duncan...

He was a wanted man. Werewolf.

Pate was searching the city for him, and Duncan was assumed to be a deadly threat.

When the power went out, six more guards had been killed in the containment facility. So many lives...lost. And all six of those men had been killed by a werewolf's claws.

Only the werewolves had been killed, too. Except for Connor. But it seemed Connor had never made it out of his cell, so he couldn't be responsible for all of those deaths.

Every sign pointed to the fact that Elias had been the one to hijack the system and take control of the collars, but he *wasn't* a werewolf. He couldn't have killed the humans in the facility.

So who had?

She knew Pate thought it was Duncan. She'd told her brother, again and again, that Duncan had been in his cell.

But he didn't believe her. He seemed to think that Duncan had escaped and gone on a rampage. He had no trust in Duncan.

And she wasn't exactly big on trusting her brother any longer.

*When did you change, Pate? When?*

Shane couldn't back her up. Because he was dead. Too much blood loss. So said Pate.

*Another lie?* Could a vampire as old as Shane die that easily, that quickly? At this point, Holly wasn't sure if Pate even knew how to tell the truth any longer.

Holly paced toward her window. It had been fixed, probably by one of Pate's men, and she stared down at the street below.

Would Duncan run? Get out of the city?

She heard the faint rustle of a footstep behind her.

Holly's eyes squeezed shut.

*He wouldn't run.*

"You shouldn't be here," she said without turning around. Her eyes opened. "You know he'll be watching my house." Her breath rasped out. "Pate thinks you killed the humans at the facility. He's hunting *you*." Her hands clenched into fists. "Leave now, before he comes."

The floor creaked.

"Please," she whispered. "I don't even know what's going on. Pate isn't the man I thought."

No one was who she thought these days.

The floor creaked again. She could feel him coming closer to her. Feel the warmth of his body seeming to reach out for her. And she could smell him. The rich, slightly wild, masculine scent that was pure Duncan.

She remembered the first time she'd seen him. He'd come into her lab. Looked so intense. Dangerous.

His fingers brushed over her arm. *Fingers.* Not paws. He'd shifted back into the form of a man.

"Holly..."

He said her name with such need.

She whirled toward him.

And saw that the wolf wasn't completely gone. His eyes still gleamed with the beast's power. His face seemed sharper than before. His cheeks more hollow. His lips a bit more cruel. And his fangs were out.

Hers weren't.

"Duncan?"

His hand rose. His fingers brushed over her cheek, and an expression of confusion flickered over his face.

"You need to leave," she told him, voice husky.

He gave a hard, negative shake of his head. "Need...*you.*"

Then his head was bending toward her neck. Holly held herself perfectly still, not afraid of him, but afraid of what was happening between them.

Their relationship was dangerous. The world around them was spinning out of control. He should be cutting town and not looking back.

Instead, he'd come for her.

His breath blew lightly over her skin. Her hands rose to his shoulders and her fingers curled around him. "Duncan, you have to—"

His mouth closed over her, right there where her neck met the curve of her shoulder. She tensed, expecting pain, a bite, but he licked her skin.

A wave of heat rose inside her.

"Need..." Duncan muttered again. "You."

And she needed him.

The sharp edge of his teeth raked over her skin, but he didn't hurt her. Had he ever?

Then his hands were on her shirt. He yanked, and the fabric tore. He tossed the material away. Shoved down her pants.

He lifted her into his arms. "Can't think of anything...else...only you."

Right then, he was all that mattered to her. "I was afraid I wouldn't see you again." Her confession.

"I'll never leave you." The promise was a man's, not a beast's.

Then they were in her bedroom. The lights were off. Like her wolf needed light to see. The mattress dipped beneath them. She expected wild, hot sex. He was coming off the full moon rush. Everyone had said this would be him at his most dangerous but...

But he was so careful with her. As if he were afraid she couldn't handle him. Silly werewolf. Was he forgetting what she really was?

His fingers pushed down her panties. Tugged away her bra. Then he was licking her. Licking her nipples. Sucking the tight peaks. Driving her out of her mind.

Her nails clawed down his back as she tried to force him to go faster. She didn't need this slow build-up. She needed him. All of him. Holly didn't know how much time they had.

But he wouldn't hurry. He parted her legs. Put one hand on each thigh.

Then he put his mouth on her.

The first orgasm caught her by surprise. Holly hadn't expected it to come so fast, but he licked her, stroked her with his tongue right on her clit, then pulled back, only to repeat that sensuous pattern and the release hit, slamming into her.

But he didn't stop. He kept tasting her. Stroking. Learning every inch of her body. When she tried to lunge up and grab him, he just caught her hands in one of his and pushed her back on the bed.

There was no stopping him. No controlling him. He was set on exploring every inch of her body.

Claiming every inch?

Her breath panted out and she took the pleasure that he gave her.

Her sex was aching, so eager to feel the surge of his cock within her. But he wasn't coming close enough to her. Damn him. "*Duncan!*"

His head lifted. He licked his lips, as if still tasting her. His eyes locked on hers. "Only...you." His dark growl.

Then he flipped her over on the bed. Lifted her onto her knees. Her hands were free, and they grabbed for the bedding, clenching around the sheets.

He was behind her. Covering her. He moved back her hair, and put his mouth on the curve of her shoulder once more. "No going back."

She arched back against him just as his teeth sank into her skin. Shocked, she cried out even as he thrust inside of her. The pain from his bite faded almost instantly as he licked over the wound, and then he was thrusting, withdrawing, driving in deeper and harder—*finally*—and the lust and need spiraled inside of her.

But...

*I know what he did.*

She knew what his bite meant. It hadn't been like a vampire's bite.

When a werewolf bit in that spot, the mark was a claiming.

The bed creaked beneath them. He felt good. Right.

Incredible.

This time, the climax built in a fast and furious rush. Her whole body tightened because that pleasure was there, just out of her reach. She drove back against him, slamming down because she wanted all of him.

He gave her all.

His hands were on her waist now. Holding her tight. Moving her so that she had to take him in even deeper. That was just what she wanted.

Her fangs were coming out. An instinctive response that didn't embarrass her. Why would it? Her lover had fangs of his own.

*I want a bite.* He'd claimed her. It seemed only fair that she get her turn. "Duncan, I need..."

"What? Anything. I'll give...anything." A promise.

Her right hand rose. Grabbed his wrist, yanked his fingers away from her waist. She had to bite him. It wasn't something that she could control. Not anymore. The urge was too dark. Too consuming. Holly lifted his wrist to her mouth.

She sank her teeth into his wrist.

"*Yes...*" His hiss.

His thrusts became even harder. She loved it. She drank from him as she came, exploding on a release so powerful that her heart seemed to stop for a moment. Her eyes squeezed shut, and the pleasure swamped her.

Duncan was there with her. Coming hard because she felt the jet of his release. Holding her, curving his body around hers. His heart didn't stop. The thunder of his heartbeat seemed to surround her. He was all that she knew in that instant.

All that she wanted.

The rest of the world could just fade away. She had Duncan.

She had everything.

His heartbeat was thundering...thundering...

And sirens were wailing.

Her eyes widened. His wrist wasn't at her mouth any longer. She didn't even know when she'd let him go. She could still taste the rich flavor of his blood. Within her, Duncan was hard again, already, but the sirens seemed so loud.

Were they coming for Duncan?

He'd tensed behind her. She looked over her shoulder. Saw the lust and need and...growing fury in his gaze.

Then he started to thrust again. The breath caught in Holly's lungs. Because now the intensity was different. So dark and focused. Consuming.

The sirens were wailing, growing ever closer, and she was staring into Duncan's eyes as he thrust deep into her.

But it wasn't enough. Not for her.

She tried to twist against him, wanting to face him fully. Needing to.

His hands locked around her. Held her tight.

He thrust harder.

She shook her head, "I want—"

*Everything.*

Then they were rolling across the bed. She ignored the screams of the sirens. This moment, it was too tense, too sharp.

She was on her back. He was between her legs. Plunging into her. Possessing her. Every stroke seemed like a brand on her. And she wanted another bite.

Wanted his blood in her. Wanted to bind them. Link them.

*I want to claim him, too.*

Then his neck was near her mouth. Her lips feathered over his skin.

"Bite." His sharp snarl.

And she did. Because she wasn't a human anymore, and the vampire that she was wanted his blood as much as she wanted his body.

The rush she got was incredible. A climax that shattered her even as the lights from the swarming vehicles lit her home.

Duncan kept thrusting. Then, once more, his release erupted within her.

Car doors slammed. The siren finally stopped wailing. Then she could hear the thud of racing footsteps.

Duncan didn't let her go.

*Run.*

The cry was in her head, but she was holding him tight.

She forced her mouth away from his throat. She could compel him to run. Make him leave. There might still be time for him to get away.

Holly looked into his eyes.

She realized that she could force him to do nothing.

"This is how they take me," he said.

She shook her head. "No."

Those footsteps were growing closer.

He pressed a kiss to her lips. "You're mine."

And he was hers.

"Don't forget it."

"*Holly*!" Her brother's cry, and it sounded as though it came from her living room.

He was going to find them together. Naked. Duncan wouldn't have a chance. "Why?" Why had he done this? Why not run?

"Because I had to be with you." His smile was a bit twisted. "Before they sent me to hell."

She wouldn't let them. Duncan wasn't going to hell. No, he couldn't—

He pulled away from her. She grabbed for the sheets even as he yanked on his jeans.

Then Pate was in the doorway. Men in black were behind him. They had their guns out. All of the weapons were aimed at Duncan and her.

"Don't shoot my sister," Pate ordered.

She jumped from the bed. Kept the sheet around her. "You're making a mistake! I told you...*Duncan was protecting us! He didn't hurt anyone!*"

But Duncan just stared at Pate, and he *laughed*. "How are you going to take me in?"

Pate's chin lifted. "The guns are loaded with silver."

Duncan moved to stand in front of Holly. "Then take your best shot, and while you're doing that..." Duncan raised his claws and said, "I'll take mine."

This wasn't happening.

"You've been playing some kind of game with us all, Pate," Duncan said, the words snapping. "I thought we were supposed to be making the world a better place, but it seems like you were just using us all, even the monsters."

The men behind Pate were looking nervous.

"What are you?" Duncan asked him as he inhaled. "Because I've noticed that you sure don't smell human."

Pate shook his head—then lunged across the room in a move so fast that he looked like a blur. Holly gasped because in less than a second's time, Pate stood with one hand wrapped around Duncan's throat and with his other hand holding a gun right against Duncan's heart.

"You're screwing things up for me," Pate bit out. "Why the hell couldn't you have stayed controlled?"

Duncan bared his fangs. "Fuck control."

And she knew, she *knew* what Pate would do even before his fingers tightened on the gun.

"No!" Holly screamed.

The gun fired.

She shoved into Duncan, knocking him aside, but the move was too little, too late.

The bullet had driven into his chest. Blood was pumping everywhere, and a sharp, acidic odor rose from the gaping hole near Duncan's heart.

She grabbed for Duncan, sinking to the floor beside him and lifting his head into her lap. Her own chest burned as if she'd taken the hit. She didn't care that her sheet had fallen away, she only cared about him.

"Don't," she whispered. Begged. "Don't leave me."

But he was. His eyes were wide, shocked, staring up at her with the glow already fading from his gaze.

She wouldn't let him go.

"Holly..." Pate's voice was sharp. He wrapped his fingers around her arm.

She stared at him with hatred. "Get the hell away from me." She didn't know him anymore. Didn't care to know him.

A muscle jerked in Pate's jaw. "You're making a mistake." He glanced over his shoulders at the men who still stood there, armed and ready to fire. "Let me help you."

The way he'd helped her before? When he'd made her become a vampire?

*Become a vampire...*

Her gaze flew back to Duncan. Could a werewolf even become a vampire? Was it possible?

"Holly..."

She used her teeth to rip open her wrist. Duncan had lost a ton of blood. Just like she had in that alley. She'd been given vampire blood when she was close to death. It had saved her.

*I'll save him.*

Pate's hand yanked at her shoulder. "Don't make me hurt you," he warned her.

"You already have." Because it seemed like he'd shot her. Her heart was breaking as Duncan lay dying.

The blue of his eyes was so weak now. His breath rattled in his chest. And he was just staring at her.

"I can't let you go," she said, staring at Duncan and knowing this was wrong but not able to stop herself. She'd just found him. Losing him wasn't fair. She didn't want to be without him.

Duncan's eyes closed.

"I'm sorry..." She put her wrist over his mouth even as she felt the press of a gun at her temple.

Pate.

"Don't make me do this." His words seemed torn from him. "Stop, Holly."

She wasn't stopping. If she had to, she'd trade her life for Duncan's because she wasn't just sitting there while he slipped away from the world. She needed him.

Loved him?

Dammit, she wanted a chance to find out.

"Pull your wrist away from him," Pate told her, voice tight and hard. "You don't know what you're doing."

"I'm saving him." And Pate wasn't shooting because maybe, deep down, past whatever twisted mess he'd become when she wasn't looking, he couldn't kill his sister.

"No." Pate was definite. "You're not. You're just making a walking nightmare."

Duncan's eyes opened. Her breath caught. She started to smile. He was coming back to her. Her blood had worked. He was—

His hands flew up and clenched around her wrist. His mouth hardened on her, and he started to suck and drink more. Harder. *Harder.*

"D-Duncan..."

His eyes stared up at her, and all she saw in that gaze was a ferocious hunger.

"We are so fucked," Pate growled. Then the gun was moved to Duncan's temple. "Let her go."

Duncan kept drinking. Taking so much that Holly began to feel weak. His hold on her wrist was too tight.

"Let. Her. Go." The gun dug into Duncan.

Duncan didn't let go.

Holly shook her head. "Pate, give me time, I can—"

He fired.

Holly screamed as her world ended.

*Ended.*

# CHAPTER ELEVEN

She had her own set of guards. Guards who watched her with careful eyes and made sure that they didn't come too close to her.

They were probably scared that she'd bite them. Considering the way she felt, Holly realized that she just might.

"Where did Pate take Duncan?" Holly asked the question for what had to be the hundredth time.

But Brent just shook his dark head. "You know I can't tell you that, ma'am."

Right. Because he had his orders. Orders that had come from her brother, right after Pate had *shot* Duncan and dragged him out of her home.

Even as she'd screamed after them.

Pate had stopped at the broken door. Glanced back at her as his men had held their guns on her. *"Trust me, Holly."*

How was she supposed to do that?

So her guards stayed. They kept their guns. While Pate had gone who the hell knew where with Duncan.

*But he was alive.* She knew that. He'd already become a vampire before Pate had taken that second shot. She'd been afraid that the transformation hadn't completed, but then she'd noticed that his wounds had been trying to heal.

She glanced down at her wrist. It had healed, too. Duncan had bit her, drank her blood, *just like a vampire.*

How did he feel now? Did he hate what she'd done to him? Being a werewolf had been bad for him, and now, well, she had no idea how he'd react to being a vampire.

"Did he go to Purgatory?" Holly asked.

Brent's eyelashes flickered, and the other guy, Henry Wells, glanced away from them.

*Purgatory.*

It was what she'd feared. But where else could Pate take Duncan? With the containment facility in Seattle shutting down, they'd have to take him somewhere else.

Purgatory was the perfect prison.

She straightened her shoulders and knew what she'd have to do. "You'll take me to him."

Brent shook his head. "Our orders are to keep you here, to keep you safe, until—"

"Until Pate comes to fetch me?" Like she was some kind of dog? Now Holly shook her head. "That's not happening." Because she wasn't going to sit back and let Duncan be punished for crimes he hadn't committed. "You'll take me to him," she said again as she pulled in a steadying breath.

She had to stop thinking and acting like she was human. She was more. Time to be more.

Brent was the weak link. He'd stared at her with pity in his eyes a few times. She'd use that pity. Because of his weakness, she knew he'd be the one to hesitate on actually firing his weapon at her.

So she went for Henry first. Holly leapt toward him and slammed his head into the nearest wall. He went down with a groan.

Brent swore and lunged toward her. Still not firing, just as she'd suspected. She grabbed him. Yanked his weapon away from him. "Sorry," she said, right before she sank her teeth into his throat.

He tasted good, but not as good as Duncan. No one was as good as Duncan. She only took a few drops of his blood, just enough to control him.

Then she eased back so that she could stare up at him. "You'll take me to Duncan." She pushed her compulsion in the words.

With slightly unfocused eyes, Brent nodded.

\*\*\*

"Sunlight is supposed to make vampires weaker, but it won't have any impact on you."

The quiet voice penetrated through the darkness that seemed to surround Duncan.

"Silver won't burn you. No matter how pure, you'll be immune to it."

That voice was familiar. Pate.

"From what I can tell, you don't have any weaknesses. Lucky bastard."

Lucky? A surge of rage pushed through him, and Duncan's eyes flew open.

He discovered that silver bars separated him from Pate.

Pate stared at him, with his arms crossed over his chest. "You'll need blood to survive, but you aren't supposed to eat the other inmates. That's frowned upon here."

*The other inmates?*

Duncan shook his head, then stopped, remembering...Holly's screams. Pain. Blood.

Fangs were in his mouth and claws erupted from his fingertips. "What did you do?"

"Not me. You can thank my sister for what you are now."

"*Where is she?*"

"Don't you want to know where you are?" Pate asked him instead.

Duncan could only glare at him.

"This wasn't the way it was supposed to be," Pate said, and damn if those words didn't sound like a broken record from the guy. "I wanted to make you strong enough, but not this way."

He wanted to rip the man apart.

Pate glanced over his shoulder, then back at Duncan. "I knew that there was a certain...power within the FBI that wasn't thrilled with the development of the Para Units. This power sent plants in to destroy us from the inside. To make it look like the monsters were taking over."

Duncan wanted to lunge forward, but he didn't move.

"Elias was a plant. I didn't know it was him at first. Hell, I thought *you* were the one that had been sent in, but then you got bitten, and Elias shot a bullet into my chest."

"And *you* shot one into my head."

Pate frowned at him. "You were pretty fucking bullet proof by then, so don't bitch and moan. We had to make the scene look real."

*What?*

"Others were watching, so even if I had to rip out my sister's heart in order to do it, I still had to put on the show."

*No one rips out her heart.*

"Elias set us all up. He followed his orders from above like a good little soldier. Those claw marks on the agents? Elias used one of the prisoners—he was working with the asshole. He got the werewolf to carve up the others for him, and that fool wolf probably thought he'd get his freedom in return." Pate's mouth tightened. "Instead, he got roasted by silver."

"How do you know—"

"We found the blood under the werewolf's claws. Elias put the guy back in his cell, all nice and tidy, but sometimes, there's blood you just can't get rid of." Pate fired another fast glance over his shoulder.

"If you know this..." Duncan's back teeth ground together. "If you know I'm clear of everything that happened, why the hell am I in this cell?"

"Because it's not over." Flat. "We have to find out who is trying to jeopardize the program. In order to do that, we needed an agent who was strong enough to survive anything that came his way." Pate's stare drifted over him. "You're the strongest thing I've seen. Even Shane can't compete against you."

"Shane's dead."

"Is he?" Pate murmured. "I'm sure that's what the villagers all thought a few centuries back, too."

What?

"An escape is going down. A damn big one. The monsters are going to be let loose, and when that happens, everyone will know what's happening here. There will be no more denials. No more secrets. Just out of control werewolves and vampires that want to feed and drain their prey dry." He sucked in a deep breath. "They've been starving the vamps, did you know that? They were supposed to be contained here, but not tortured because we can be fucking humane, or at least, we *should* be."

Duncan didn't speak.

"But someone wants it all to fall apart. Someone wants the Para Units to look like failures, and that same someone—that power that is *in* the FBI—wants the monsters loose so the humans can see them all at their worst."

"Why?"

"Because I'm thinking he—or she—wants a war. An all-out battle. An annihilation. When humans find out about the monsters, how do you think they'll react? Will they stop to see who is good, who's bad?" Pate shook his head. "No, they'll see fangs. They'll see claws. And they'll attack. The paranormals can't compete with the humans, not in numbers, and they'll all die."

But it would be bloody. A massacre of both humans and paranormals.

"We won't let that end game play out." Pate's voice was hard.

Duncan narrowed his gaze.

"All of the most dangerous, most powerful paranormals are here. But they aren't getting out. No matter what plan is in place, you will stop it."

The guy had to be insane. "Just me?"

Pate stared back at him. "Just. You."

"You know I won't survive. I'll die here."

"No, you *can't* die. Not any longer."

Right. Like he was supposed to believe—

"You're a werewolf, *and* you're a vampire. You don't have the weaknesses of either, but you've got the strength of both. You're the only paranormal of your kind in existence. Hell, most would say you *shouldn't* be able to exist."

Duncan didn't have a ready comeback.

"I told you before...you're an alpha, and that's what paranormals understand. You go deeper into the prison, you face the bastards who think they're in charge, and you damn well wipe the floor with them." Pate's shoulders heaved. "*That* will get the others to follow you. You'll find out who's helping to stage the escape. You'll stop it. Hell, man, you'll wind up saving the world."

"Why me?" Duncan demanded. "And why the hell didn't you tell me all of this sooner?"

"Because I didn't trust you at first. I'd planned to do the deed myself. I'd even been getting injections of Shane's blood so I'd be stronger, but then you had to get yourself bit." Pate exhaled. "That sure changed up all the plans in place."

"You were using me."

"I'm fighting to keep this world safe," Pate said, holding his gaze. "Sometimes, the things I have to do aren't always pretty."

"You're a bastard, you know that?"

Pate nodded. "That's what Holly told me when I took you away."

*Holly.* "Where is she?"

"Do the mission, and I'll tell you."

*Sonofabitch.* Duncan surged forward and found himself right in front of Pate. The silver bars—he'd ripped them away. "How the hell...?"

"Told you," Pate said, rocking back on his heels. "Only strength. No weaknesses."

The bars fell from Duncan's fingers.

"Now do the job. Stop the escape, and if you want, I'll even damn well sing at your wedding to my sister, but we have to stop this nightmare first. *Do you understand?*"

Duncan wrapped his fingers around Pate's throat. "I understand that you've been using me."

Pate's eyes widened.

"And I understand that I don't fucking trust you." How many lies had Pate told him? "You *shot* me."

"Only after you'd taken Holly's blood."

He remembered the sweet taste of honey on his tongue. No, not honey. Better. So much better. He'd gorged on that taste. *I want more.*

"If I hadn't shot you, then you wouldn't have stopped drinking from her." Pate tried to pry Duncan's fingers from his throat. "I saved her."

Had he been hurting Holly?

Duncan released Pate.

Pate didn't back away. "In five minutes," Pate said, "a guard will come in here for you. He'll take you to general population. The werewolves there are supposed to all have collars and the vampires aren't let out during the night. During the day, the vamps will be as weak as humans. Controllable."

"I won't be controllable," Duncan said.

Pate shook his head. "No, you won't be." He raked a hand through his hair. "I'm hearing rumors that the vamps are being starved and the werewolves are being tortured by silver—all to make them angrier, to get them ready to fight back against their guards." His face was haggard. "We have to stop this. Will you do it? Will you stop the escape and help me figure out who's pulling these damn puppet strings and trying to start a war?"

It looked like he didn't have much of a choice. "Holly's safe." Not a question, a demand.

"Yes! I left agents at her place to keep an eye on her. She's protected, okay?"

A light scent teased Duncan's nose. Sex and honey. In hell. He gave a sharp negative shake of his head.

"What?" Pate barked. "What is it?"

"Holly."

"She's—"

"Here." His snarl. Pate had betrayed him for the last time. He would cut the bastard open.

"That's not possible!"

"I smell her." Not just her sweet scent, but also her fear. Holly was there, and she was terrified.

Footsteps echoed, the tread coming toward him. The prison guard that Pate had spoken of?

A growl built in Duncan's throat.

"Let him take you into the general population," Pate whispered. "Do it. Dammit, I've got a mole in this prison, and he told me we don't have much time."

"Why didn't he tell you who was behind the setup?"

"Because he's a weak werewolf, the runt of this joint, and he doesn't have that kind of power."

Duncan inhaled again on a deep breath. "*Holly.*"

"Are you fucking sure?"

The guard was almost on them.

Duncan nodded.

"I'll get her," Pate promised. "I'll search the prison, and I'll get her out, I swear. Just do this mission. You can't even imagine how many lives are at stake."

He could imagine plenty. Only right then, there was only one life that mattered to him.

Holly's scent was coming closer because the guard was coming closer. The guard had been near her. Near enough for Holly's scent to recently rub off on him.

*My senses are even more enhanced.*

Duncan held Pate's glittering stare. "I'll get her," Duncan said, "and I'll end this fucking mission."

Pate wouldn't use him again.

Pate didn't get a chance to reply. The door opened, and the guard came in. A middle aged, balding man, he froze when he saw the broken bars—and Duncan.

"It's all right," Pate said. The director had a gun in his hand. When had he pulled that out? "I have him contained. Just collar him, now."

With trembling hands, the guard hurried forward and snapped a collar around Duncan's neck. When the guard lifted his hands...that was when Duncan noticed the fresh puncture wounds on the man's neck.

Holly's scent was coming from those wounds.

Just what was his vampiress doing?

"S-supposed to collar him," the guard said. "Bring him in..."

Was it his imagination or did the guard look dazed?

The collar snapped in place. Even though the silver was glowing, Duncan didn't feel a burn. "Come with me," the guard said, lifting the collar's remote.

After one final look at a tense-faced Pate, Duncan followed the guard out. They walked through a series of hallways, past heavy, silver doors. Duncan caught the salty scent of the ocean, drifting in to him from the windows high above.

"Werewolves aren't allowed out during full moons. So you'll be locked up tight then," the guard told him.

The full moon had just passed. Duncan had survived that night. Well, partially, and he wasn't exactly planning on hanging around the prison until the full moon came calling once more.

"The werewolves are housed on the south side. The vampires on the north."

Since he was supposed to be some combination of both, where did that put him?

"But you're due for an infirmary check first. Got to make sure your collar's strong enough to last, but not strong enough to kill you."

Uh, yeah, that was good.

Then the guard was motioning with his weapon. Pointing toward a door on the right. "Ten minutes in the infirmary."

Was this standard protocol?

"The doctor's waiting," the guard muttered, looking away.

*His* doc?

Duncan shuffled forward. The door to the infirmary opened, and she was there. Wide eyes. Red lips. Face so fucking beautiful that she'd haunt him forever.

"Is he secure?" Her voice was flat.

"Y-yes..." The guard stammered.

She turned those deep eyes on the guard. "Then stand outside the door. Don't let anyone in while I'm with the prisoner."

She reached for Duncan's arm. Pulled him inside. She shut and bolted the door behind him. The guard didn't say a word.

Then her mouth was on Duncan's. Just the touch of her mouth against his seemed to ignite a firestorm inside of him.

He'd thought he'd lusted for her before, but now every sense was heightened. Every emotion raged out of control.

He wanted to bite her so badly that his teeth ached.

Her tongue thrust against his. He loved her taste. Would never get enough of it. Couldn't get enough of her.

*Mine.*

The beast was still inside him, but that claim came fully from the man.

Holly pulled her mouth from his. "I was afraid I'd lost you." Her words were hushed. He could hear the whisper of pain in her voice. Her gaze was stark as she stared up at him. "I'm so sorry, Duncan."

He wanted to speak. Couldn't. Because he could hear the wild thunder of her heartbeat. *Want her blood.*

"I shouldn't have given you my blood. I know you didn't want to change."

His gaze was on her throat. On the pulse that raced so frantically.

"But I couldn't let you die." The words broke. "Please, Duncan, say *something*."

He put his hand on her neck. He had claws. The claws of a werewolf came from his fingers. But he didn't scratch her skin. He didn't want to waste that blood. "Mine."

"Wh-what?"

He pushed her against the wall. Trapped her. "Mine," he said again, then his mouth was at her throat. This was instinctive, primal. There was no stopping, not now, not with her, though a part of him watched from a dark corner of his mind, horrified at what he was doing.

*Can't stop. Must take.*

Her hands pushed against his chest. Before, her vampire strength would have been enough to send him stumbling across the room. Now, he barely felt the push of her hands.

His mouth was on her throat. He licked the skin. She trembled.

He bit.

When her blood flowed onto his tongue, it was the best thing he'd ever tasted. Better than wine. Better than honey. Better than any damn thing. His cock hardened even more because he'd been aroused since the moment he'd seen her. It stretched, ached, and he yanked down her jeans and shoved aside her panties even as he kept drinking from her.

The bloodlust tangled with the physical lust that he felt as he shoved down the uniform pants he wore. He wanted to speak, to tell her that he didn't want to hurt her, but he couldn't pull away.

With one hand, he lifted her up. Held her easily, then drove deep into her. She moaned against him and arched—not away from him, but toward his mouth.

Oh, fuck, but he hoped she was enjoying his bite. Because nothing could have made him pull away from her right then.

Her sex contracted around him, so tight that his cock felt like it was gripped in a silken fist, and he thrust deep into her even as he drank her blood.

He should have been repulsed by what he was doing.

He fucking wasn't.

She came around him. He swore that he could taste the pleasure in her blood as her body tensed and she choked out his name.

Then, only then, was he able to take one last sip from her. He swiped his tongue over the wound on her neck, and he came so long and hard that his body shuddered.

The fury of need slowly faded. Pleasure still pulsed through him, small aftershocks as his cock emptied into her. Her arms were around him. Her legs locked around his hips.

He was almost afraid to look at her. He'd been worried that she'd think of him as a beast before, but he'd just damn well *gorged* on her. She'd chased after him, apologizing, and he'd done *that* to her.

Careful now, when he should have been careful before, Duncan eased out of her. Her breath caught, and his gaze flew to her face.

There was no anger in her eyes. No pain. Just the afterglow of pleasure.

He stared at her. Lost.

How the hell could she still look at him like that?

Then she smiled at him. *Smiled*. She said, "You aren't going to...ah...believe this..." Her voice was breathless, husky, and it just made him hard again, "but I promise, I came here to save you, not just to fuck you."

Right there, in the middle of Purgatory, with death all around, with fangs in his mouth and claws growing from his fingertips, he...smiled.

Her breath caught. "Duncan, you've got dimples."

He kissed her. Not wild. Not desperate. Just...kissed her.

Her lips whispered back against his.

"I'm sorry," he told her softly. She deserved so much better than what had happened.

"For what?" She shook her head. "Duncan, I'm the one who changed you."

And he was the one who'd just attacked her.

His forehead pressed against hers. "You shouldn't be here."

"I wasn't going to let you just be tossed into some cell and locked away." Her nails sank into his shoulders. "I can get us out of here. I just have to bite the guards, then I can control them. They don't realize I'm a vamp, so they aren't taking precautions and—"

He realized why Pate had kept Holly's secret for so long. Because Pate had known that if the dark segment within the FBI found out about her, Holly would be watched, monitored, and maybe even tossed to the wolves for the battle that was coming.

*Good thing this wolf found her.*

"I'm not leaving."

His quiet words froze her. Then she gave a hard shake of her head. "You have to leave. Look, I know your brother is here, but you can't stay. You haven't done anything wrong!"

He hadn't done anything right, either. "Connor's here?"

She gave a slow nod. "He was transferred in, the same day you were. I...convinced one of the agents to tell me that. Brent had quite a bit of information to share." Her gaze searched his. Her legs had slipped away from his and fallen back to the floor. The scent of blood and sex surrounded them.

*Want more.*

He forced himself to step away from her. She wouldn't be able to handle him taking much more from her.

But when he stepped back, she blinked and almost looked hurt as she fumbled to fix her clothes. Then her hand rose to her neck.

"I'm sorry," he whispered again.

Her hand dropped. "I just...I couldn't let you die."

"And I'm not going to let my brother die." Because Connor would die. With the battle coming to this prison, all of the inmates were at risk. Some would escape, some would die.

"He's a killer, Duncan. He deserves to be here, but you don't."

He could still taste her. Duncan turned away from Holly. Straightened his clothes. His fangs hadn't gone away yet. Why not? "He was taken away by whoever the hell it was that killed my family. I remember him screaming for me, but I was locked in that closet, and I couldn't get to him."

There was silence behind him.

"I'll get to him this time." A vow. "He'll tell me what happened to them. To me."

"And then what? You get him out, and you two walk into the sunset together?" Her laugh was bitter. "You're a vampire now, and he's a werewolf. He's also out for your blood."

He glanced back at her. "I'm not leaving him." That was all he knew for the moment. He'd find Connor, and then...well, he didn't know what would happen after that. "According to your brother, this prison is set to erupt in a matter of hours."

Her eyes widened.

"Elias was a plant. Someone wants the Para Units to fail, and that same someone wants Purgatory to fail."

"But if the prisoners get out of Purgatory—"

"Then Pate thinks a war will come. He says the vamps have been starved. That the werewolves are too close to losing their control. They'll get out and go wild." Because they had the baddest, most dangerous prisoners there. "He didn't bring me here as punishment. He brought me here to stop that hell from coming true."

Her lips parted in surprise even as she took a step forward. "I'll help you."

"No." Absolutely fucking not. "You'll use your power over the guard, and you'll get him to take you out of here. *Now.*"

"So you can fight them all on your own? You can't do that. You're just—"

"According to Pate, I'm the only vampire and werewolf hybrid in existence. All of the strengths of both creatures, none of the weaknesses."

A furrow appeared between her brows. "Alpha..."

So he'd been told. He just hadn't realized what that meant at the time. He was betting that Pate had known though, all along. Tricky bastard.

"That jerk," Holly whispered. "He set this all up."

Duncan suspected he had.

"So what? You're supposed to take on all the prisoners here by yourself? That's insane!"

"Not all of 'em...just the asshole who thinks he's in charge." Because there would be one leading the pack. There always was. Once Duncan took him down, the others would follow.

Or at least, he hoped so.

"I can *help* you."

He shook his head. "No, you'll make me weak."

Her indrawn breath was painful, and dammit, he hadn't meant the words that way, but they were the truth. Physically, he was strong. Amped up paranormal, yeah, he had that whole bit going on. But Pate was wrong when he'd said that Duncan didn't have a weakness.

He was staring at his weakness. "If one of them gets to you, I'll lose it." The painful truth.

"Duncan..."

"You matter to me." Mattered so much that he was *glad* she'd transformed him. Because the transformation meant that he had a chance to be with her. Not just for a few years, but maybe forever. "If I thought you were in danger, I don't think I'd ever be able to hold onto my control." He huffed out a hard breath. "So don't stay, understand? Use the guard and get the hell off this rock before the battle comes." Then he went back to her. Because he had to. One more time. "I'll find you. We'll both be more than just monsters." A man. A woman. Maybe with a future?

The wound on her neck had already healed. He could feel her, though, inside of him now. "Get out and stay alive." *For me.*

She nodded.

His shoulders wanted to sag in relief. Instead, he kissed her once more. Had to do it. Then he headed for the door.

"Don't you want to know why?"

He'd unbolted the door. Duncan didn't glance back at her.

"Aren't you a little curious..." Holly pressed. "About why I couldn't let you die?"

"No." Because he already knew. Duncan shoved open the door. "You love me."

And he...well, he was insane for her. Obsessed. Consumed.

To him, she was everything.

That was why he had to leave her. If anyone at that prison realized how important she was, he'd be lost.

Not an alpha. Not the warped hero who was supposed to swoop in and save the unsuspecting humans out there.

If anything happened to her, he'd just be...lost.

Because the vampire who'd bit him held his heart in her hands.

\*\*\*

When the doors closed behind Duncan, Holly didn't move for an instant. Her clothes were back on. She'd thrown away her torn panties. Her body was still flushed, and pleasure still pulsed within her.

She couldn't move.

Duncan was walking away. He knew how she felt, and he was just leaving her.

*Because I'm his weakness?* She wasn't sure how to take that. She'd come there, so desperate and breaking every rule she'd ever known, in order to save him.

Now he'd told her to leave.

The door swung open. Brent stood there. "The guard took Duncan to general population."

She was supposed to just leave him?

No, she couldn't do that. She'd stay out of the fight. He could go play alpha, but when the bloodbath was over, he'd still need someone to get him out of that hellhole.

She'd sworn not to leave him behind, and she wouldn't. No matter what.

Holly cleared her throat. "Go find my brother. Bring Pate to me." The control was so easy to her now that it was frightening.

Brent nodded and hurriedly left.

She stared at the infirmary around her. She'd need some sort of weapon, just in case. Everyone in this place seemed to have fangs and claws, and her compulsions wouldn't work on other vampires.

She jerked on a lab coat. If any other guards came by, she wanted to make sure that she blended well. She searched around a moment, and then Holly picked up a scalpel. Silver. She wondered why the doctors had silver scalpels in stock. Actually, now that she looked at the instruments, they were *all* made out of silver. Odd. Silver surgical instruments would just increase the pain for the werewolf patients.

Did someone want them all to hurt? The thought chilled her.

But hadn't Duncan told her that the vampires were being starved? Pate had billed this place as being a humane place to hold the dangerous non-humans. She clutched the scalpel tightly. Just what was happening in Purgatory?

"I thought I smelled something sweet."

The dark, low words had her stiffening. She shoved the scalpel into the pocket on the right side of her borrowed lab coat, then spun around.

She'd expected to see a guard. Because prisoners shouldn't be wandering loose, right? Some asshole, horny guard who thought he'd make time with the new female doctor.

But...a man in a dark gold prison uniform stared back at her. He wasn't alone. Two others, wearing the same matching prison uniforms, were behind him. The man in the middle was big, about six foot three, maybe four, with dark black hair that had grayed slightly near his sideburns. His face was hard, so rough, and his eyes—

*They looked just like Duncan's.*

The same glowing, bright blue that his gaze became when the beast ruled him. She could even see the shining flecks of gold in the center of this man's eyes.

His eyes were like Duncan's, but his face was an older version of Connor's.

She'd been right. Duncan's father hadn't died all of those years ago.

Hadn't died, but he sure might have *killed*.

"You shouldn't be here," she said, lifting her chin and trying to brave her way through whatever the hell was happening.

He inhaled. "Vampire." He said the word the way some men might say...*chocolate*. Like he was about to savor a treat.

Her knees locked. Her fangs burned. "Get out."

He smiled at her. "Vamp females always have a certain scent but you...you don't just smell like a vamp." He stalked toward her. His gaze raked over her. "There's wolf all over you."

There was about to be silver *in* him if that jerk didn't back off. "Guards!" Holly yelled.

He laughed at her. "You don't know how things work around Purgatory, do you?"

Duncan couldn't be that far away. Had he heard her yell? She hadn't really yelled for the guards. She'd yelled so her lover with his enhanced hearing could pick up her cry.

"Smells like you've been fucking in here."

Her face seemed to ice.

"Nothin' like fucking a female vamp...except of course...killing one." Then he lunged toward her, with his claws up.

She brought up her scalpel and didn't waste her breath on another yell.

# CHAPTER TWELVE

The werewolves were housed in the south section. The vampires were to the north. At least, that was the spiel that the guard had given him.

*Where are you, Pate?*

The heavy, silver doors slid shut behind Duncan, and he found himself in a big, cavernous room. Dozens of men walked around, but they all froze when they saw him.

Not men. Werewolves.

Every single one of those guys wore a glowing silver collar. Collars all just like his. Pate's little invention had sure been shopped around.

So this was the general werewolf population. Only he wasn't seeing Connor in that mix.

His gaze drifted up. The cells were on the second level. Silver cells to imprison them when it was time to lock up the monsters again. Guards walked along that second level, guns gripped tightly in their hands. No doubt, those guns were filled with silver bullets.

Growls reached him. Snarls of fury. His gaze turned back to the werewolves. The group was closing in on him, and some of those faces were familiar.

*I put some of them here.* Shit.

"*You*," snarled a werewolf on the right. Judd Orton. A werewolf who'd slaughtered five women on the coast. "I dreamed of slicing you open."

Duncan shrugged. "Better me than the humans you attacked."

"*You're dying!*" Judd jumped toward him. His claws were out and the silver was burning his neck.

Duncan punched him, driving his fist right into the werewolf's face. Blood spurted as Judd's nose broke, and Judd flopped to the floor, screaming.

The other werewolves stopped advancing.

"*Alpha...*" A low whisper that came from another convict that Duncan recognized. Charles Rist. He'd enjoyed killing children. That twisted freak should *never* see daylight.

Duncan let his gaze sweep over them all. "Who's next?"

Charles came for him. Running and snarling, even as smoke rose from the burning skin on his neck. He swiped out with his claws, slicing Duncan across the stomach.

And Duncan swiped out with his own claws. He gutted Charles, and the werewolf fell to the ground, screaming.

Duncan expected shots to rain down on him from above, but when he risked a quick look up at the guards, they hadn't moved.

*What the hell?*

But he wasn't about to lose focus. "Next," Duncan said, and it was a demand.

Only no one else stepped up. Their gazes were on the moaning Charles, and then, one by one, the men lowered their heads.

"Alpha." Clear. A growl from them all.

Duncan stood before them, body tense and ready for battle. "Why aren't the guards attacking?" His voice was low, designed to carry only to the paranormals near him.

One man, a werewolf Duncan had never seen before, glanced up quickly at the guards, then his gaze darted to Duncan. The werewolf looked young, barely over twenty, and his face was so pale. "They like to watch us fight each other."

What?

"When we kill each other," the young werewolf continued, "that's one less prisoner for them."

The werewolves were backing away from Duncan. Slinking away. No more challenges? This was too fucking easy.

Only the pale werewolf was lingering. "You're gonna be dead soon," he said as he swallowed. He licked his lips. "You...you don't want to challenge for alpha."

Challenge for it? Hadn't he just damn well won the title? The competition had been slim.

But the werewolf crept closer even as Charles crawled away. "They weren't saying you *were* alpha...they were saying...s-saying they'd let the alpha take you out."

Oh, really? "So where the hell is he?"

"He...he sliced open the last new werewolf and went with the guards to the infirmary. They...they let him do whatever he wants. He said..." The werewolf glanced over his shoulder. "He smelled something sweet in the air and w-wanted a bite."

The thunder of Duncan's heartbeat echoed in his ears.

*Something sweet.*

There was only one sweet thing in Purgatory. And he'd *left* her in the infirmary.

"The last werewolf," Duncan forced himself to speak. "Did you get his name?"

A fast shake of the guy's head. "He went down too fast. Alpha...the alpha knew him. Said h-he'd finish him this time."

*Fuck, fuck, fuck.*

Duncan spun away and ran back for the silver doors that had sealed behind him. He shoved his fist against those doors. "Let me out!" He had to get back to the infirmary. Back to Holly.

She'd said that she would leave. *Be gone. Please, be gone.*

The door began to dent beneath his hammering fists. Guards shouted for him to stop. Oh, now they were getting involved? Screw that.

The escape was supposed to go down at any time. They were cutting it to the wire. The alpha was *gone*. Duncan was betting that his trip out of general population had been perfectly timed so the fellow could work on the escape. Like there'd be an escape without the alpha's permission.

*Don't be near Holly. Don't. Be.*

And he was in the wrong damn place. If he'd just stayed with her for a few more minutes...

The plan was screwed.

He kept pounding with his fists. Started to carve up that metal with his claws.

"Stand down!" A shout from above. Duncan guessed they'd just realized the silver wasn't working to control him. "Stand down, or we *will* fire!"

Let them. He had to get out of there, and if it took some silver bullets to the back in order to get the job done, he was ready for the pain.

Holly was in the infirmary. He suspected that Connor was there, too. *He sliced open the last new werewolf.* If Duncan needed to bleed in order to get his ass taken there, so fucking be it.

He slammed his fists into the door again.

And the silver bullets slammed into his back.

\*\*\*

"You bitch!" But the words were said with admiration. Admiration? The werewolf with Duncan's eyes stumbled back and yanked the scalpel out of his shoulder. He'd been too close for her to hit his heart.

*Next time.*

The doors swung open behind him, and guards came in. Gray uniformed, *armed* guards. "Help me!" Holly cried out. "The prisoners are—"

They were dragging someone in behind them. A man with blond hair. His prison uniform was soaked with blood.

He moaned, the sound heavy with pain.

Connor?

"Leave him," the werewolf—*he shouldn't have Duncan's eyes*—snapped to the guards.

They dropped Connor and turned for the door.

"Stop!" Holly shouted at them. "Help me!"

But they kept going.

And the big werewolf laughed as his men grabbed Connor's body and tossed him onto the nearest gurney.

"Helping you isn't on the agenda for tonight," the werewolf told her. "Those men...they know they need to get someplace safe and hunker down if they want to survive the night."

She jumped back. Grabbed another scalpel. She held it in front of her. "Who are you?"

He tilted his head. "Isn't it obvious?" He lifted his hands. "I'm the alpha, and I'm gonna be clawing you wide open." His gaze drifted to Connor. "Just like I did to my sorry excuse for a son."

*Son.* She'd already known that. Her fingers clenched around her weapon.

"The monsters are breaking out tonight, and I'm leading them to freedom."

His men laughed behind him. They were blocking the door. Locking her in.

"I just needed an excuse to be brought here. Attack the new werewolf, get him so injured he had to be brought to the infirmary...and, of course, the guards were only too eager to do my bidding."

"You attacked your own son?"

"Not like it's the first time." Anger tightened his face. "Fool thinks he has what it takes to be alpha. Only Con never had the killer instinct."

"Y-you do."

He leapt toward her. Shoved aside the table she'd stupidly hoped would be some kind of protection. "Yeah, I do." His gaze fell to the scalpel. "Where you gonna shove that one?"

"I was thinking in your heart."

He smiled. "Let's see how that works for you."

She would have to be fast. Because she knew he was planning to sink his claws into her this time. If he took her head, then—

The infirmary doors swung open.

"I told you to stay the fuck out!" The big werewolf bellowed as he swung around.

Only this time, the guards were different. Not the quick-to-obey men before. *Men who'd been working with the werewolves.*

These guys looked shocked to see the werewolves in the infirmary, and they immediately drew their weapons.

Immediately wasn't fast enough. The wolves close to them attacked. Holly screamed as the humans went down, fighting desperately.

And the man that they'd been transporting, the man on the gurney that lay so still, he was dropped to floor in the middle of the attack.

*Duncan.* So bloody, so—

Duncan leapt off the floor. He sliced into the two werewolf flunkies, sending them flying away from the humans before they could go in for the kill.

The humans were bloody, unconscious, but still breathing.

Duncan rushed toward the other werewolf. Then, just a step away from him, Duncan froze.

Holly's heart was thundering in her chest. Duncan's eyes had widened as horror washed over his face.

"Well, well..." The werewolf was smug. Shocked, but smug. "Knew I'd find you again someday, son."

"You..." Duncan's voice was hoarse.

"Ian," the werewolf said. "Name's Ian, and I've been looking for you a very long time."

She was just *standing* there. Screw that. Holly ran toward Connor. The breath hissed from between her teeth when she saw the damage that had been done to him. He needed to transform in order to heal from those injuries, but he'd lost so much blood that she feared he was too weak for the shift.

"He's already dead," Ian said, without looking at her. "Boy was always useless. Always fucking crying." He crept toward Duncan. "For you. He thought you'd come and save him."

"Y-you killed my family." Duncan sounded lost, almost like a child.

Holly started trying to apply pressure to Connor's wounds. If she could stop the blood flow...

Connor's eyes opened. His hand flew out and wrapped around her wrist.

"I *am* your family!" Ian roared this. "That bitch of a useless mother tried to take you from me. I found you, and I made sure she never betrayed me again!"

"Her blood..." Duncan's voice was a whisper. "I was in her blood. It ran under the closet door."

Ian swore. "I *knew* I smelled you in that house, but the cops were coming. I had to hurry."

Connor stared up at Holly. There was so much rage, no, hate, in his stare.

Then Connor's gaze cut to Ian and Duncan.

"And here you are...at the perfect moment." Ian's voice rose. "You can help me. We can take over this prison, bust out, just like I planned, and then we'll make the humans all fucking sorry."

"How'd you plan it?" Duncan asked, and his voice held no emotion.

Connor was nearly breaking her wrist. *Been there, done that once already.* She'd prefer not to have the bones snap again.

"I got connections...thought gettin' tossed in here was the end for me. I didn't realize it was just the beginning."

"No." Duncan shook his head. "It is the end. For you." His shoulders pushed back. There was so much blood on him, but he didn't seem to be weak in any way. "I remember you."

"Do you?" Ian's claws were at his sides.

"I remember hearing my mother scream. She was begging for you to stop."

Ian laughed. She hated his laugh.

"I remember the sound of my brother's voice, asking me to help him."

Ian was still laughing.

"I was too afraid to move then. Too afraid to speak. My mother had told me to stay quiet. No matter what happened...*stay quiet.*"

Connor was lifting Holly's hand toward his mouth. His claws sliced her skin, but she bit her lip, refusing to cry out. She knew what he wanted.

What Duncan wanted.

She was trying to help them both.

"I'm not going to be quiet any longer." Duncan smiled at Ian, and the sight was chilling.

Her blood dripped into Connor's mouth.

"The first time I saw Connor, I knew he looked familiar. But it was your face that I was really starting to remember." Then Duncan jumped forward. His claws wrapped around Ian's throat. "You took my life away."

Ian didn't look scared. Didn't act scared either. He drove his claws into Duncan's side.

Holly screamed and jerked away from Connor.

But Duncan didn't so much as flinch from the attack. "I'm not some little whelp that you can kick around any longer." His fangs were lengthening. "I'm the alpha now, and you're just the killer that needs to be stopped."

A low hiss filled the air. And Ian's chilling laughter sounded once more. "You think I'm alone in this?"

The gas drifting from the vents was just like the backup security system that Pate had installed at the containment center in Seattle. Was this where Pate had gotten the idea? Or had he taken steps to have his system also installed here?

She covered her mouth, but the gas didn't seem to be doing anything to her. It wasn't even stinging her throat.

Connor was motionless on the gurney.

"The gas is the first wave. Only it's not taking out the paranormals. It's gonna knock out all the humans. Then it won't matter who has the controls to the fucking collars. It won't matter who has the silver bullets. The guards who aren't already paid off will fall, because the others—the ones working with me—they'll be the ones in gas masks running for the doors."

Holly's gaze flew around the room. There were no controls to the collars in there. There were more surgical instruments though, against that back wall. She could rush over there and get more silver to help Duncan.

"Who set this up?" Duncan rasped.

But Ian wasn't looking at him any longer. Ian's bright blue gaze had come to rest on Holly. "What did you make him?"

She wouldn't, couldn't, speak.

"I tried to get a vampire to convert me once, but the bitch wouldn't do it."

Good for her.

"So I cut off her head."

Not so good.

"If you cut off *her* head, Connor, I'll take you back."

What?

Then she felt the hand on her shoulder. Connor, not so still anymore. Standing right behind her. She could feel the press of his claws on her skin.

"Kill her," Ian ordered, "and you can walk out of here with me. All will be forgiven. We can start fresh." His gaze darted to Duncan. "My two sons. We'll fucking rule this new world."

"The new world?" Duncan repeated. "You mean the world where you start attacking the humans."

"We've lived in the shadows long enough!"

"No, you've just *lived* long enough."

Connor wasn't attacking her. Whatever he'd done, she didn't believe he was like his father.

Neither was Duncan.

She broke away from Connor. Grabbed for the scalpel on the back table. *I can't let his father's death be on him.*

Some sins shouldn't be carried.

Duncan yelled her name, but she didn't stop. Her fingers were tight on the scalpel, and she moved as fast as she could. What good was being a vamp if you never used your power? So she amped up her power and moved faster than she'd ever moved before.

It seemed like everyone around her was moving in slow motion. Connor was lunging for his father with bared fangs.

Duncan was reaching for her.

Ian was smiling.

Smiling...

And lifting a weapon she'd never seen. A wooden stake that had been tucked in his prison uniform.

So even as she stabbed down with her knife— slicing over the bastard's throat—he shoved that stake into her heart.

"Told me...be ready." Blood spurted down the front of Ian's throat. She hadn't cut the bastard deep enough. "Vamps...coming..."

And the slow motion ended for her. She sank to her knees and stared at the stake hanging from her chest.

She felt the cold whisper of death on her skin. The same whisper she'd felt in that alley, a year ago. Goosebumps rose on her even as a strange numbness filled her extremities.

Duncan was shouting for her, and she wanted to answer him, but she couldn't.

The gas kept filling the room. The stake—it had slammed into her heart.

She knew it had found the mark because her heart had stopped beating.

*I'm sorry, Duncan.*

She'd just wanted to protect him, but now, it looked like she'd just left him to face his nightmare without her.

*I'm sorry.* Her lips formed the words, and then she could say no more.

Ian's claws came toward her, and she knew he planned to take her head.

# CHAPTER THIRTEEN

*I'm sorry.*

He couldn't hear the words, but he could read them on her lips and they ripped right through him. Duncan shoved his father aside—*his father, his fucking father*—and grabbed for Holly.

Her eyes were sagging closed. Blood pulsed from her wound. No, this couldn't be happening. Not to her. He'd left her in the infirmary so that she'd be safe.

Not so that she could be staked while trying to fight his past.

"Vampires. For all their strengths, they can still be so damn weak." Disgust had thickened Ian's voice.

*You have no weaknesses.* Pate had promised him that, but the guy had been wrong.

He had a weakness. She was bleeding out in his arms.

A dull roar filled his ears. His hand was on her throat, trying to feel for a pulse, but nothing was there. "Holly?" He shook her.

Her eyes weren't opening.

"*You won't leave me!*" He whispered the desperate words to her.

She hadn't let him slip away, and there was no way that he'd let her—

Claws pressed into his back. Sank into his spine. Twisted. The agony burned through him, but he didn't let Holly go. He couldn't.

"Worthless piece of shit," Ian snarled into his ear. "You think I didn't smell you all over her? I knew..." His claws yanked out of Duncan. Drove in again. "I knew you were linked to the bitch. Mated to a vamp."

*Mate.* Yes, she was his mate. She was everything.

"I just had to get to her..." Now the claws were at his throat. "In order to make you weak. Just like *he* said..."

The claws were about to slice across his jugular. His father's claws.

*Stay in the closet, baby. No matter what happens...stay in and stay quiet.* In his mind, Duncan saw warm golden eyes, swimming with tears, staring down at him. *Mommy loves you.*

Love.

Holly wasn't moving.

"Who. Said." The snapped words didn't even seem to have come from him.

Ian still had his mouth near Duncan's ear. "You thought you were stopping us, didn't you? But when you started hunting the paranormals, he got smart to you. He's *in* your precious FBI, and he's not gonna let his own kind be caged."

*"Tell me who the fuck he is."*

"He's a werewolf, an alpha, just like me. We're gonna rule. Gonna make the humans scream.

Putting us all together was a mistake. Now we're just stronger. We're—"

"Get the hell away from him!" Connor's scream. The enraged roar of a man, but for a moment, Duncan could have sworn that he heard...

*Help me...help me, Duncan!* The cry of a child.

Ian was yanked away from him. His father and Connor met in a fury of fists and claws.

Duncan's fingers wrapped around the stake in Holly's chest. The stake wouldn't kill her. Well, she wouldn't *stay* dead, not unless she lost her head or her body was burned. As soon as the stake came out, she'd heal.

He ripped that damn stake from her. Smashed it into bits.

Her eyes flew open as she sucked in a deep breath.

His Holly. His world.

He bent his head. Pressed his lips to hers. "I love you." Because she needed to know that. "Now, please, stay here. Whatever happens, don't move."

*Stay quiet.*

Because he didn't want her in the line of fire.

Duncan looked up. Ian had Connor pinned against the far wall, and the older werewolf was going for Connor's throat.

Gathering all his strength, Duncan lunged across the room. Before Ian could slice open Connor's throat, Duncan caught his hand. "That's my brother," Duncan said as his body vibrated with fury. "And you *aren't* hurting him anymore."

Connor's gaze flew to Duncan. There was disbelief and wild hope fighting in his stare.

His stare...golden just like their mother's had been.

*I remember him now.* From the moment that he'd seen Connor in that basement, the memories had started to push through the shadows in his mind. *My brother.*

Ian whirled to attack Duncan. His father had yanked the silver scalpel out of his chest and he drove that scalpel right toward Duncan's heart.

And the bastard was smiling as he did it. "Let's see you save someone now, hero." The scalpel sank into Duncan's chest.

Duncan glanced down at the weapon. "Isn't it supposed to burn?"

Ian's face paled.

Connor had fallen to the floor, but he was trying to stand once more.

"I think it's supposed to burn." Duncan's fingers wrapped around the handle of the scalpel. "Or at least it would, if I were just a werewolf. But I'm not."

And silver didn't hurt vampires.

*All of the strengths. None of the weaknesses.* Pate hadn't been bullshitting after all.

So he pulled out that scalpel. Saw his blood dripping from it. "You destroyed my life that night."

"She took you away from me! My flesh! My blood—"

The blood kept dripping from the scalpel. "It is your blood." Duncan glared at him. "But I'm not you."

Ian attacked with fangs bared and claws out. Kill or be killed. The way of the wolf.

Duncan wasn't in the mood to die.

So he twisted his hand and pushed the scalpel into Ian's heart, and this time, it did burn. Ian screamed. He clawed at his chest, but Duncan just drove the weapon in deeper. Smoke rose from Ian's chest.

When Duncan finally stepped back, Ian hit the floor. His features were frozen in a final mask of horror. Shock.

Death.

"I'm not you," Duncan said again. His mother had protected him from this monster. Given her life to keep him safe.

Duncan's gaze rose to Connor. The other wolf was shuddering, but he was back on his feet. His wounds seemed to be closing.

Was he going to have to fight another battle? Duncan had just killed his father, he didn't want to kill his brother, too.

"You..."

"I wish I could have saved you," Duncan said, when Connor's voice just trailed away. "I wish you'd been in that damn closet with me."

Connor looked away. "You don't...remember it all, do you?"

No.

"I-I was supposed to go in, but I was afraid of the dark." His voice was hushed. "Mom told me that you would keep me safe inside, that we had to be quiet, but I was afraid." He swallowed, and the small click was painful to hear. "So I ran out, screaming. That's how he found us. He heard my scream. He killed her when she was reaching for me, and he took me away."

Hell.

"I'm sorry," Duncan said. Sorry for the life that Connor must have lived. For all the pain and suffering he'd endured.

"So am I." Connor stared at him. The lines on his face seemed so deep. "I wish I'd stayed with you in the dark."

"Duncan?"

His head turned at Holly's call. She stood there, blood on her, but *alive.*

He ran to her and pulled her close. She was trembling against him, and he knew her body was weak. *Because she'd been fucking staked.* "Drink from me," he ordered as he forced her mouth to his neck.

He'd never forget seeing her so still.

His hands tightened around her as her teeth sank into his throat. The pleasure of her bite rocked through him. Holly. His Holly.

*His.*

Always.

Her tongue whispered over his skin as she fed lightly from him. "Take more," he said.

*Take everything.*

The gas was still leaking from overhead. The humans would be down. They'd need help. They'd need—

The infirmary doors burst open. Duncan spun to face the new threat, shielding Holly with his body.

But the new threat was just Pate. With...Shane standing behind him. Pate had a gun in each hand. So did Shane.

Pate's gaze raked the room, then landed on him. "Thought you might need a hand," Pate said.

"He's alpha..." These soft words came from Connor. "He doesn't need anyone."

Yes, he did. He needed Holly.

Shane approached Ian's body.

"He's the one who was working the escape from inside the prison," Duncan said, voice flat. "He was also my father."

Shane hissed out a breath. "And who put the silver in his heart?"

Holly's fingers stroked over Duncan's chest, as if she were trying to soothe him.

"I did," Duncan told him.

Shane nodded. "It's a bitch when the worst monsters are the ones who made us." He turned away from the body. "Know how you feel. I had to take my father's head in 1396."

Thirteen—

"Did he tell you who was helping him on the outside?" Pate demanded. He hadn't put his weapons up yet.

"Uh, you think we can work on turning off the gas?" Holly asked, and Duncan loved the slight snap in her words. "If Ian was telling the truth, it's knocking out all of the humans."

Pate finally put up his guns so that he could yank out a radio from his coat pocket. A few seconds later, he started talking to someone. Brent?

"Turn it off," Pate ordered. "Now."

The gas shut off. An alarm sounded.

Pate lowered the radio. "We're on lockdown," Pate said. "You, Shane, and I need to secure the prison and make sure no one gets off this island."

"Just the three of us?" Duncan nodded. "Right. Piece of fucking cake."

"I can help," Holly said.

And he knew she could. Holly was strong. She was fierce.

But she was also more than just a killer, and they needed her skills. "The wounded are gonna come in. You'll have to take care of them." Because there was no telling how injured some of the guards—and prisoners—would be.

Her gaze slid to Connor. "I'll start with him," she murmured.

His Holly. A healer, not a killer.

Holly flashed her fangs. "But if you need me, you yell, and I'll have your back."

Or maybe, maybe she was both.

Duncan pressed a kiss to her lips. He loved her little fangs. Hell, he loved everything about her.

"I love you," he said the words against her lips and felt the surprise that rippled through her.

Holly shook her head.

He caught her chin. Forced her to look straight into his eyes. "I love you."

Maybe he'd been falling for her from the very first day—when she jabbed a needle in his arm and took his blood.

His Holly...always after his blood.

But he'd known for sure how he felt about her when he saw Holly lying so still on the infirmary floor. When her heart had stopped, his had, too.

Her lips began to lift in a small smile.

"Uh...we've got an island full of blood-thirsty monsters. A prison gone wild. Get your horny hands off my sister and *follow orders*, McGuire."

Duncan spared a glance for Pate. "When this is over, I'm marrying her."

Pate raised one brow. "When this is over, you'd damn well better."

What?

"Did he tell you who was helping him?" Pate asked as his eyes cut to Ian's prone body.

"No." There hadn't been time to force answers. Only time to live or die. "We just know that he's in the FBI, someone high up, and that he's a werewolf."

Pate's eyelashes flickered. "That's more than enough."

"You know who the bastard is?"

"No, but I know how to trap him now, and for the moment, that's good enough."

There was no more time for talk then. They could hear voices crying out in pain and screaming for help. They ran out, and Duncan looked back just once before he followed Pate.

Holly was beside Connor. Helping him lie down on a gurney.

Saving his brother.

Just as she'd saved him.

\*\*\*

She stitched up the humans and the werewolves. Gave bagged blood to the vampires who needed it in order to survive.

Two men died. Humans. Guards who just didn't wake up from whatever gas Ian had sent pumping through the ventilation.

Five other guards were caught—all wearing gas masks—as they tried to leave the prison.

Now they were the prisoners. Held in a cell just beyond the infirmary.

"Bite them," the order came from Pate, but it wasn't an order he gave to her. Holly glanced up and saw Shane closing in on the men. "Make them tell us everything they know."

Holly eased out a slow breath. Compulsion. Pate wasn't going to stop until he had his answers.

He glanced over at her. His eyes narrowed on her face. "Don't."

"Don't what?" She tossed away her bloody gloves. All the patients had been tended to. Or at least, she'd done what she could. More guards had been flown in on choppers, more doctors, too.

Things were under control in Purgatory, for the most part.

"Don't look at me like I'm a stranger," Pate said. There actually seemed to be pain whispering in his voice.

She realized that was exactly the way she'd seen him. "I don't know you anymore."

He turned and caught her hands. Behind him, she saw Shane enter the cell with the guards.

Pate said, "I never wanted to risk you, not in any way."

"But you'd risk Duncan?" Because he had.

"I had a job to do. More lives that you can guess were depending on me."

"That doesn't make Duncan expendable."

Pate shook his head. "No."

"Were you setting him up all along, just so that he'd be strong enough to fight whoever was waiting in this prison?"

Pate searched her eyes. "He wanted you. I saw it in his eyes the first time he looked at you."

That wasn't an answer to her question.

The infirmary doors squeaked open behind her. *Duncan.* She knew it was him without even looking. She could smell him. Feel him.

"You wanted him, I saw that, too, but you weren't going to risk being with a human. You thought you were too dangerous."

Her hands clenched within his grip.

"I knew what potential Duncan had inside of him, and I knew that if he was going to be with *my* sister, then he'd have to be strong enough to protect her."

She didn't want to hear this. She'd asked but—

"I made him strong enough."

Insane. Cold-blooded.

Pate's eyes cut over her shoulder. "You're welcome, McGuire. Don't worry, you can thank me later."

Pate began to stalk past them.

Holly's hand flew out. She grabbed Pate's arm. "You owe him."

He shrugged. "I owe a lot of people."

"You *owe* him, and you're gonna pay." Even if she had to make him do it.

"And just what payment is it that I owe?"

"Let his brother go."

"*What*?" Duncan and Pate said at the same time.

Then Pate shook his head. "That man is a killer. There's no way he's leaving this island."

Duncan had fallen silent once more.

"What if he's not a killer? What if he's not the man you think at all?" Because she'd seen a different side of Connor. He'd been in the infirmary, and he'd *helped* her work on the prisoners. He wasn't a cold-blooded killer, she was sure of it. "Check him out. Dig deeper. Find out the truth about him. If he's not the man you think, then *let him go*."

Pate stared down at her. A tense moment passed, then, "You know I'd do anything for you."

Even force her lover to become more than human? Yes, she was getting that idea. That terrifying, horrible idea.

Pate nodded grimly. "I'll dig deeper. Shane can compel or you can or—"

"I can," Duncan growled. "I'll be the one to find out my brother's secrets."

"Fine." Pate exhaled on a rough sigh. "If he isn't the killer we think, he'll go free. You have my word."

Then Pate was walking away. Holly reached for Duncan's hand.

"Oh, Duncan, just so you know..."

Pate had stopped near the guards' cell. Shane was inside. The guards weren't moving.

Duncan frowned at him.

"I was bullshitting before. Getting you amped before the battle. I *do* know your weakness, and I'm not talking about the desperate need you seem to have for my sister." Pate glanced back at him. "If you ever hurt her, I'll make everything that's passed before this moment seem like a fucking cake walk for you. Got me?"

Duncan's fingers twined with Holly's. "I got you." He didn't sound scared, though.

Pate grunted and entered the cell.

Duncan's attention turned back to Holly. "I got you," he said again, the words softer.

They were in a prison for paranormals. She was a vampire. He was, well, *alpha*, but she'd never been happier than she was in that moment. "You won't ever hurt me," she said, absolutely sure of that.

"No, I won't." His lips feathered over hers. "I'll just love you, for the rest of my life."

He kissed her again, then he was pulling her from the infirmary. More federal agents were there. She knew that Pate had hand-picked all of those agents. She and Duncan passed them all, went outside, out into the darkness that waited.

But the darkness could be beautiful. She'd learned that fact. And monsters...

They weren't all evil.

In fact, some of the monsters were actually heroes.

They climbed onto the boat. A boat that would take them away from Purgatory.

*We'll get you out, too, Connor.*

She knew they would, just as she knew her instincts about Connor weren't wrong. The mission wasn't over, not completely, not yet.

But they'd keep working until Connor was free, and until the werewolf working *against* the Para Units had been stopped.

The boat cut through the dark water.

Duncan pulled her close. "I love you," he whispered.

She'd never get tired of hearing those words from him, and, since they both now had unnaturally long life spans ahead of them, she figured she'd be hearing those wonderful words plenty of times.

She'd died, lost her humanity, but found it again—with him.

She'd found hope. She'd found love.

She'd found her alpha. A man with a wild side that she adored.

Howls drifted on the wind behind them, and his arms tightened around her. Before them, the night seemed to stretch endlessly.

There was nothing for them to fear in the dark.

Holly smiled and knew that her fangs would flash in the night.

# EPILOGUE

Pate stared at the werewolf and vampire who sat across from him. The werewolf was sweating. Only to be expected. This would be his first mission and his first chance to start earning some redemption.

"You understand the mission?" Pate asked carefully. Someone was trying to start a war between the humans and paranormals.

It was Pate's job to stop that war.

By any means necessary.

Connor nodded quickly. "Y-yes."

"And you'll do what I say, follow the orders you're given without question?"

Another nod.

"Good." Despite what he'd learned about the werewolf, Pate still didn't trust him. Not completely.

But then, he didn't trust anyone completely. Except for Holly.

Pate's gaze cut to the vampire. The oldest vampire he knew, and one that had cheated death more times than should be possible. "And you're willing to take the risk?"

Shane smiled, flashing his fangs. "Purgatory will be a walk in the park."

No, it wouldn't be. But there were more answers to be found in that prison. Answers that he thought the vampires there could give to him.

He just needed a strong vampire to find those answers.

A vampire and a werewolf.

Because sometimes, it took monsters to save the world.

"Then, gentlemen, let's get started..."

**THE END**

# A NOTE FROM THE AUTHOR

Thank you so much for reading THE WOLF WITHIN.

If you'd like to stay updated on my releases and sales, please join my newsletter list.

*https://cynthiaeden.com/newsletter/*

Again, thank you for reading THE WOLF WITHIN.

Best,
Cynthia Eden
*cynthiaeden.com*

# ABOUT THE AUTHOR

Cynthia Eden is a *New York Times*, *USA Today*, *Digital Book World*, and *IndieReader* best-seller.

Cynthia writes sexy tales of contemporary romance, romantic suspense, and paranormal romance. Since she began writing full-time in 2005, Cynthia has written over one hundred novels and novellas.

Cynthia lives along the Alabama Gulf Coast. She loves romance novels, horror movies, and chocolate.

**For More Information**

- *cynthiaeden.com*
- *facebook.com/cynthiaedenfanpage*

# HER OTHER WORKS

**Trouble For Hire**

- No Escape From War (Book 1)
- Don't Play With Odin (Book 2)
- Jinx, You're It (Book 3)
- Remember Ramsey (Book 4)

**Death and Moonlight Mystery**

- Step Into My Web (Book 1)
- Save Me From The Dark (Book 2)

**Wilde Ways**

- Protecting Piper (Book 1)
- Guarding Gwen (Book 2)
- Before Ben (Book 3)
- The Heart You Break (Book 4)
- Fighting For Her (Book 5)
- Ghost Of A Chance (Book 6)
- Crossing The Line (Book 7)
- Counting On Cole (Book 8)
- Chase After Me (Book 9)
- Say I Do (Book 10)
- Roman Will Fall (Book 11)
- The One Who Got Away (Book 12)

## Dark Sins

- Don't Trust A Killer (Book 1)
- Don't Love A Liar (Book 2)

## Lazarus Rising

- Never Let Go (Book One)
- Keep Me Close (Book Two)
- Stay With Me (Book Three)
- Run To Me (Book Four)
- Lie Close To Me (Book Five)
- Hold On Tight (Book Six)
- Lazarus Rising Volume One (Books 1 to 3)
- Lazarus Rising Volume Two (Books 4 to 6)

## Dark Obsession Series

- Watch Me (Book 1)
- Want Me (Book 2)
- Need Me (Book 3)
- Beware Of Me (Book 4)
- Only For Me (Books 1 to 4)

## Mine Series

- Mine To Take (Book 1)
- Mine To Keep (Book 2)
- Mine To Hold (Book 3)
- Mine To Crave (Book 4)
- Mine To Have (Book 5)
- Mine To Protect (Book 6)
- Mine Box Set Volume 1 (Books 1-3)
- Mine Box Set Volume 2 (Books 4-6)

## Bad Things

- The Devil In Disguise (Book 1)
- On The Prowl (Book 2)
- Undead Or Alive (Book 3)
- Broken Angel (Book 4)
- Heart Of Stone (Book 5)
- Tempted By Fate (Book 6)
- Wicked And Wild (Book 7)
- Saint Or Sinner (Book 8)
- Bad Things Volume One (Books 1 to 3)
- Bad Things Volume Two (Books 4 to 6)
- Bad Things Deluxe Box Set (Books 1 to 6)

## Bite Series

- Forbidden Bite (Bite Book 1)
- Mating Bite (Bite Book 2)

## Blood and Moonlight Series

- Bite The Dust (Book 1)
- Better Off Undead (Book 2)
- Bitter Blood (Book 3)
- Blood and Moonlight (The Complete Series)

## Purgatory Series

- The Wolf Within (Book 1)
- Marked By The Vampire (Book 2)
- Charming The Beast (Book 3)
- Deal with the Devil (Book 4)
- The Beasts Inside (Books 1 to 4)

## Bound Series

- Bound By Blood (Book 1)

- Bound In Darkness (Book 2)
- Bound In Sin (Book 3)
- Bound By The Night (Book 4)
- Bound in Death (Book 5)
- Forever Bound (Books 1 to 4)

## Stand-Alone Romantic Suspense

- Never Gonna Happen
- One Hot Holiday
- Secret Admirer
- First Taste of Darkness
- Sinful Secrets
- Until Death
- Christmas With A Spy

Made in United States
North Haven, CT
20 March 2024